QuIt MonKs or DIE !

QUIT MONKS OR DIE!

A NOVEL BY MAXINE KUMIN

STORY LINE PRESS

1999

Published by Story Line Press, Three Oaks Farm, PO Box 1240, Ashland, OR 97520-0055

This publication was made possible thanks in part to the generous support of the Nicholas Roerich Museum, the Andrew W. Mellon Foundation, the National Endowment for the Arts, and our individual contributors.

Dust Jacket by Lysa McDowell
Cover photo by CORBIS / Dan Lamont
Text design by Michelle Thompson

Library of Congress Cataloging-in-Publication Data

Kumin, Maxine, 1925-
    Quit monks or die! : a novel / by Maxine Kumin.
        p. cm.
    ISBN 1-885266-77-4 (alk. paper)
    I. Title.
    PS3521 .U638Q58   1999
    813'.54--dc21   99-20971
                                                                          CIP

Quit Monks or Die!

ACKNOWLEDGEMENTS

I am indebted to Deborah Blum, whose book, "The Monkey Wars," provided the factual background for this story, and to James A. Kaplan, M.D., former Medical Examiner for the State of New Hampshire, who authenticated the medical evidence.

I

DREW DEVERAUX was in his mid-forties. Wiry, bandy-legged and ferret-faced, he moved even now with the macho grace of a cowboy, a man who has met and overcome rampaging cattle, invading coyotes and blown down fences. He woke on Easter Sunday morning in his apartment on Quincy Street, a scythe-shaped sweep of three rooms over a bodega and a flower shop on one of Napara's quieter downtown corners. No bars, no furtive sales of controlled substances taking place under the sodium lights.

St. Vincent's Hospital stood cattycorner to the bodega. The wails of ambulances coming in at all hours punctuated Drew's nights. Since he slept only fitfully, he found the throbbing notes oddly comforting. Others were in equal or worse pain. Others, too, were looking death in the teeth.

He got up slowly, rubbing at the bone aches along his spine, where new tumors were doubtless erupting like baby teeth. Three years ago the surgeons had lifted a fat loop encrusted with tumors out of his intestine and sewn the pieces back together. Three months of chemo, of puking and lassitude, had thrust him back into the misery of his childhood, a long, lonely road.

Always, though, he put up a good front. "Just keep that fucking priest out of my room," he'd said to Joanna during the first hospitalization.

Joanna Hammerling, a highly regarded sculptor in metal, who was, come to think of it, his best friend, unwrapped a stick of Juicyfruit gum with her big knobby fingers. Drew bit down on it gratefully. Gum and quartered lemons; they were as much as he could tolerate.

"He gives me the creeps tiptoeing around in here. Preparing me to meet my maker. If I'm gonna die, I want to do it my way."

"What's your way?"

"I don't know yet, do I? But no mumbo jumbo."

"Kicking and screaming, you mean." She had marched into the nurses' station, he could hear her command growling all the way down the hall. "Mr. Deveraux does not wish to be absolved, confessed, forgiven, or saved. No clergy to be admitted, is that understood?"

Once the treatments were over he gradually came back to himself. He could taste food again, appreciate the sweat on the outside of a good cold beer. The surgeons had done a clever job of resectioning. Thank God he didn't have to wear a bag.

He was back to work and in the clear for almost two years before the crab bit into his liver. They took half of it out. Livers were amazing; they could regenerate. The blood tests every six weeks for invasive cells were negative. Life, even without another swallow of beer, now forbidden, began to seem possible again. He'd left Graysmith and gone to work at Joanna's, helping with the welding now that most of the animals were gone and he was off stable duty. He fussed around the studio, kept the grounds tidy, but she could see that everything was an effort. He wasn't sorry when she decided to hire a kid to help out.

Before he'd taken the custodial job at Joanna Hammerling's ranch, Drew had been head maintenance man at the Graysmith Lab. He'd wetmopped miles of tile floors, scrubbed urinals and toilets, scoured graffiti off stall doors and performed a dozen minor repairs to stuck windows and broken chair legs. When the top floor was converted to animal research, blood began to appear in Drew's stools. And when he went on sick leave after the surgery, his boss found an excuse to replace him with this spic Manuel something, a greaser he could put on the payroll for two bucks less an hour than Drew had been pulling down. Man-well; even the name was a reproach. Not that he gave a rat's ass that the guy was Mexican and spoke with an accent. He himself was Cajun, though the only French he had retained was *merde* and *foutoir*. But it was lousy this poor slob was getting screwed just so the rich Jew director could put more gas in his new BMW.

That rich Jew director, though, had been better to his mother than he had been. Every time he came home to make a fresh start with Lottie she ended up hitting the bottle again. She knew it was poison, she said so whenever she was sober and sometimes she was sober for long stretches. But she couldn't keep it up. Hadn't he beaten her up a couple of times when she was crazy drunk out of her mind? And wasn't Lottie drunk a circus act gone to hell?

For that matter, when he got a couple of beers in him, didn't he go a little crazy himself? *Only spics use knives,* he'd said once to some faceless guys in a bar; he had no respect for that kind of brawling, preferred his fists in a fair fight. Well, that was long ago and far away, when he'd been a real working stiff, not this broken down herring-gutted fool.

Even before the kid she'd hired was in place afternoons and weekends, Drew moved out of Joanna Hammerling's bunkhouse to the apartment in Napara. He told Joanna he needed to be close to St. Vincent's since he planned to die there. But he promised her that he would come by often, that he was on call whenever she had something for him to do.

In the beginning he would have said she was the kind of rich-bitch eccentric he despised. Rich enough to buy her way into the best breeding stock, rich enough to summon the priciest vets, pay top dollar for the fanciest frozen semen. But there wasn't anything she wouldn't do for her animals, and, as time went on, for him. She was the salt of the earth. If he could have said the word *adore*, he would have said it about her. The only time that word got used in his experience was in church, where you adored the Almighty. If you went to church. He'd given it up years ago.

Now, though, he was pissing blood. He'd been pissing blood all week, unwilling to face further tests. The doctors had told him the most likely site for a reappearance of the cancer was in his testicles. He was goddamned if he'd let them cut off his balls; he'd die first. Now, watching the toilet bowl turn gently pink again, he gave a short sardonic bark. He *would* die first. He was going to die.

By habit, he looked out the bathroom window to the alleyway. Was his truck still there? The rate cars got stolen these days, he was wary. He did a lot of cruising around lately, driving with the bench seat pushed back as far as it would go to ease the nagging pain in his gut; he had to stretch to reach the pedals. There wasn't an east-west, north-south cowpath within a forty-mile radius that Drew hadn't investigated. He knew the inhabitants of every paddock: every donkey, quarter horse, Texas longhorn steer, ostrich or emu — these monster birds were getting popular with ranchers desperate for a quick killing — he noted the condition of stockades and barbed wire fences, the presence of antennae and dish satellites, the peelings of paint from otherwise sound houses, the presence or absence of hay stored in pavilions.

When nothing else came right for him, he got behind the wheel and drove. With the worsening discomfort in his midsection he cruised around a lot at night, just to pass the time. Into Montandino, up and down the ever-so-discreetly tended tree-lined streets that seemed to him to ooze contentment through pores in the blacktop. Up into the foothills of the canyons in the blackest nights, across and through the desert, skimming it like a great bird of prey. He wore a goddamn map of the area inside his skull.

He leaned a little ways out the bathroom window. The old black pickup was in its slot. Not that it was worth diddley squat, but it ran, it got him where he had to go.

Which today was to Joanna's, a forty-five minute drive to the desert. They'd have Easter dinner together, former employer and former employee, two solitaries who'd been through several griefs together. The mystery virus that wiped out her llama herd. The wrangle over old Hammerling's estate, which was mercifully settled in her favor. His own mother's final alcoholic decline on the streets of L.A., the sad final trip to identify her body in the morgue.

Drew knew he looked like shit. The mirror gave back a jaundiced face, a deep haggard look about the eyes. But he could count on Joanna not to pry. She knew he was hanging on by his fingernails. Meanwhile, there would be baked ham with pineapple. There would be Louisiana yams caramelized the way Lottie used to make them in the good old days. There would be sweet New Orleans jazz piping through the artfully concealed speakers as two old friends partook of a meal together.

II

EASTER WAS DYED EGGS and chocolate rabbits for the kids after Mass and a heavy Sunday dinner Anglo style, only roast lamb instead of goat. It was all part of *una viða mejor*, the life his parents had crossed the border for twenty years ago and gone to work in the strawberry fields. Manuel Agosta had been ten years old and terrified that night, scrambling up the slope beyond the river and through the fence, though now they were all legal, with green cards since the amnesty. He was head of a household, he had social security and health insurance, which was why he stayed in this dead-end job. He prayed to Jesus that he hadn't gotten Maria pregnant again last night. He had tried to interrupt, the way he always tried, but feared that he hadn't succeeded.

Promptly at seven Monday morning he unlocked the front door of the Graysmith Behavioral Sciences Lab building, walked dreamily up two flights of shallow concrete steps and inserted his key in the door that opened onto an array of steel cages housing Dr. Baranoff's monkeys. From the moment they heard his footsteps they set up their usual melodic hooting and chirping. They were hungry and thirsty, they were restless and unhappy. Some of them were rightfully fearful; these were the ones that had been prisoners in the hole. "The pit of despair," he had heard it called. He couldn't imagine how the lab assistant assigned to the case could calmly sit there taking notes as the poor creature struggled to climb up the metal sides of the pit. Eventually of course they always stopped, out of exhaustion and despair, and the elapsed time was noted on their chart. As was how many more hours or days went by before they ceased responding to the human hand that slid the top grating open every eight hours and offered food. Eventually the monkey just curled up on the dirt bottom; this was called entering a catatonic state. Once they got this far they were removed, but it was usually hopeless. Most of them came away crazy from the experience.

Manuel always tried to spend a little time with each one, for wasn't he too in a cage of sorts, trapped in a minimum-wage job, with a wife who worked for wages as a domestic, with three kids being looked after by his wife's mother with her ignorant peasant ways, her superstitions and prejudices? He hung up his key ring— thanks to God he'd been able to replace the lost key before Dr. B. discovered it missing— and started down the aisle.

His eye took in the empty cage before his brain understood its import. The cuddly little squirrel monkey and her baby that had only arrived a week ago were not there; he rejoiced to think that they had somehow escaped. The lab was switching from rhesus macaques to squirrel monkeys because they were cheaper and smaller, easier to handle. Manuel loved the looks of the new import with her button nose and intelligent brown eyes. The baby appeared to be so frail; he feared it would never survive the impending separation.

How could they be gone? And then the incident of the key connected with the cage door ajar on its hinges and the beautiful young daughter of the Director swam back into his head. He knew what had happened. But what to do about it?

Why couldn't this have happened while his predecessor was still on the job, that bantam-weight fighter with the foul mouth and the good heart? Mary, mother of Jesus, everyone who knew this Drew person could see he was dying. But why hadn't this happened while he was still custodian? He would have known what to do.

He worried all the way down the line, methodically cleaning one cage after the other, chirping to the tenants, handling the tame ones, trying to reassure the terrorized ones. Only after he had scrubbed out the floors, refilled the water pans, distributed the monkey chow, only then did he go to the phone.

Of course he knew Diego, they were of the same race, if you could call it that. They attended the same church, they were partial to the same foods, but Manuel found him a forbidding personage. It was the uniform, the power, the handcuffs clipped to his belt, the gun holstered on his hip. Never had he dialed this number before. The taste of fear was sour in his mouth.

III

Diego — Digger — Martinez, Montandino's Chief of Police, was enjoying his midmorning coffee and forbidden sugar doughnut — he was supposed to be cutting down on fats — when the call came. He sighed the patient sigh of a man who is often sorely tried but always capable of coping. After all, a decorated veteran of World War II, a thirty-year veteran of this job as chief in a somnolent little town in southern California, a still vigorous man of seventy-three dead-set against retiring, need not hurry through his break time.

The Chief was a man of modest height and impressive girth. He had a full head of steel-gray hair, which grew forward from the crown, and a luxuriant mustache still only lightly tinged with gray. His eyes, the dark brown of his ancestors, were set well apart and bulged slightly, giving his face a startled but intelligent look. Chewing and swallowing gave him time to think. Who'd have risked breaking into Graysmith? Clearly it was the work of an animal rights type, and ever since Carla Strombaugh came last fall, Montandino had plenty of those. Hadn't his own wife got the fever with her bumper sticker: Lab Animals Never Have a Nice Day?

Digger rested his hefty forearms on the desk. For some reason, while he'd been enjoying his coffee break, his brain was busy with the image of Drew Deveraux careening all over town in his battered truck, running away, Digger thought, from his life sentence. They weren't exactly friends, but they knew each other well, through a dozen chance encounters over the years in all the likely places.

When Joanna Hammerling's house was broken into. When three of her llamas got loose on the highway. When Lottie collapsed at the Baranoffs'. When a couple of teenage kids from good families, imitating some of their peers in neighboring Napara, experimented with peyote and had to be hospitalized; it was Drew who hauled them in, having stumbled on them hallucinating wildly out near Joshua Tree Monument.

The two men knew each other well enough to have exchanged some significant confidences: that Digger, all those years in the Navy, was secretly hideously queasy and even on occasion violently seasick but always managed to attribute his bouts of puking to something in the food. That Deveraux, who rode at least a hundred broncs in his rodeo days, was mortally terrified of horses. He let on only that he respected them, but even as he grew older riding the range on sincerely docile quarter horses, fear shadowed him as he sat in the saddle, the picture of nonchalance.

Duende was the word for it. *Duende* was what Digger had acquired over the last three decades. Montandino was his town now. He had lived here just about as long as any of the town fathers. He was a California chauvinist, like those Easterners who come to the state and immediately enroll in a wine-tasting course. Digger wasn't a wine drinker, but he had developed his palate for the hang, clutch and smell of California, most particularly for the aroma and feel of this dry countryside verging on desert.

You didn't have to be an Anglo anymore to belong here. He had run the gamut. He had been called a spic, a greaser, a Mexican nigger, a Chicano. Now he was something to brag about, he exemplified ethnic diversity, a Latino, the Latino Chief of Police, someone to be prized and deferred to.

Well, this was a pretty kettle of fish. The break-in had to

be premeditated; Manuel had said there was no sign of forced entry. An inside job, then, one of the grad students connected to Graysmith? Not too likely. Dependent on Baranoff's good will, they pretty much toed the line. Baranoff could hire and fire, nail any miscreant by black-listing him from this behavioral lab or a half a dozen others around the country where he was well known. Just not likely that one of his own would defy him.

The Chief gave a little involuntary shudder as he fore-saw the scene when Baranoff was told. The whole town was in awe of Dr. B., who had swept in from the East some-where— New York, Digger remembered— to take over a dormant scientific facility and singlehandedly turn it into a world-class institution. At least in the eyes of Montandinians it was world class. The Director, who could charm and scream almost in the same breath, who had in one dozen years secured millions of dollars in grant money from the federal government, who had brought jobs and even fame of a sort to the town, had Montandino in thrall. Sinister thrall now, given the publicity his animal experiments had garnered.

But there would be hell to pay, all right, about the break-in. There would be a senior-sized tantrum. Heads would roll, salaries would be reconsidered, leaves cancelled. If he had access to a brig, Dr. B. would throw all of them in it. The Chief sighed and heaved himself out of his chair. He guessed he'd better get over there.

Manuel was right. No sign of forced entry. An inside job. He wrote both these facts down in his notebook and logged the time as well. It was useless to dust for finger-prints; too many hands opened and closed these doors. Maybe the empty cage door? But the thin metal strip didn't leave enough of a surface to hold prints. Otherwise, that might have been worth a call to the forensic lab they used.

When they used one. Last time, about a year ago, trying to pick up prints on a stolen car, they had recourse to the lab, but the prints they found weren't on file. These wouldn't be either.

Although a simple break-in didn't require it, he put in a call to the state police. The nearest unit, he knew, was out on Route 287, where the Monday morning volume of traffic invariably produced an injury-related accident or two. If it wasn't sun glare, it was fog; if it rained, cars hydroplaned all over the place as the roads filled with water. Nothing ever drained in this part of the country.

While he was waiting for the dispatcher to shuffle some squads around and free up a car, Digger inspected the premises. He was very familiar with the first floor of Graysmith, which housed the lab's famous experimental education project. The nursery school and kindergarten rooms had been home to his own Aurelia thirty years ago. Now grad students her age observed the kids and studied the things they did, the toys they played with, the things they said to each other, and wrote long, learned papers about them. It was the psychology of this and the psychology of that; he couldn't see much sense to it. Kids are kids, after all.

Not much had changed. The same off-white walls, the same appealing primitive paintings made by four- and five-year-olds, the same dollhouse corner, ditto a massed collection of blocks, ditto enough trikes and wagons to fill a warehouse. Outside, every kind of playground equipment, even grander than he remembered. What was the word they used? Enrichment.

Privately, he thought that these kids were too enriched. Growing up a desert rat in Arizona in the thirties, he'd played in the dust with sticks gathered from the arroyo. These kids had stacks of miniature logs that locked together, and diagrams to show them how to build a fort, a cabin, a horse barn. He'd clambered up on rocks to be an Indian scout. These kids had a treehouse, monkey bars, swings and slides, seesaws, a huge turntable, even a tunnel leading to a fake cave. Nothing much left to the imagination, was how Digger saw it. He remembered how the arroyo had filled with a torrent when it rained, how he was warned to stay away from it, for children drowned in it every year, how there were mysterious frogs to be found there and how, for a few days, a stubble of green grew along the banks. You were a jungle explorer discovering alligators and dinosaurs. You went inside yourself and used your imagination.

While he was waiting for the state troopers, Digger cruised around the outside. He admired the plantings designed to soften the lab's fortress-like appearance. Its poured concrete walls, three storeys high, looked pretty forbidding in this landscape. Several fan palms, bright yellow and red hibiscus, clusters of flowering crabapple and plum trees surrounded three sides. Camellias bloomed everywhere. Various citrus trees were heavy with fruit. There was a narrow band of well-watered grass through which dandelions were determinedly poking. Beyond this strip of lawn, a wide circle of chapparal growth was left undisturbed.

The lab grounds extended for at least a quarter mile in every direction. He hadn't walked the perimeter in years. The day was benevolent, still cool enough to be comfortable. The troopers would take their own sweet time; he might as well have a bit of a walk. Theresa was always after him to get more exercise. It would make up for the doughnut.

Just to rule out the possibility that the missing monkeys had wriggled free from their kidnappers and were foraging somewhere nearby, Digger decided to walk in concentric circles about fifty feet apart. He had gone maybe a quarter mile and was beginning to sweat pleasantly when he saw the grating. Had there been a well here once, long ago? The

plywood under the grating looked fairly new; its lamina-
tions hadn't begun to separate. Someone had covered this
well in the last year or so, was his guess. He tugged the
grate off and upended the plywood. At first he thought he
had found nothing more than a dry hole, perhaps dug as a
well and then abandoned. But then he noted that the sides
were reinforced with steel plates.

Something caught his eye; a glimmer of light reflected
off a piece of metal? He unhooked his flashlight from his
waistpack, knelt down with some difficulty and fumbled it
on, then shone it down the metal sides to illuminate the Rolex
watchband on the corpse of the Director, Dr. Harold
Baranoff.

IV

CHANNEL 77 in Los Angeles had recently moved into new offices. The deep burgundy carpeting still smelled of chemicals, the banks of fluorescent lights cast a gentle desert-like glow on the ochre walls. A Muzak version of Vivaldi played in the background as doors opened and closed with the sucking sound of the tide ebbing. It was a windowless interior, at once bland and terrifying, with corridors that led to discreetly guarded interview rooms, a makeup studio, and a cozy theater for the preselected studio audience.

Carla had made the four-hour drive almost in a trance. She had reserved a ticket to the Geraldine Huckaby talk show at the last minute, unsure if she dared reimmerse herself in the world she had left behind. The desire to be present, physically present, in the same building as two of The Mercy Bandits was overwhelming. She didn't expect to encounter any of her old co-conspirators — it had been several years — and even if she did, she reasoned, her own appearance was so dramatically altered she would not be recognizable. For one thing, she was thirty pounds lighter. Her hair, once long and permed into fuzzy ringlets, was now bobbed in a straight cut, layered in back. Then, she wore flowing dresses designed to disguise her bulk. Now, she dressed in jeans or leggings, with skinny tops. Still, it was eerie, unnerving, to come this close to the heady and violent days of her past.

To gain access to the theater she had to produce her ticket and personal identification. Her driver's license listed Carla Strombaugh, 5'2", 106 lbs., brown hair, green eyes, birth date 7/7/1951. Ever since the assassination on stage of one young man by his former lover, all entrants to the Huckaby audience were required to pass through a metal detector. Carla told herself that this screening was merely an airport passage, she was just another safe body in transit. But the barred gates and electronic detectors of the women's correctional facility in Illinois where she had done time created a shiver of recognition.

Geraldine Huckaby had made a name for herself hosting flamboyant characters ranging from drag queens to depressed housewives to confessed child abusers. Since the murder, she was trying to restore her image with talk shows that contained redeeming values even while they centered on controversial public issues. Today, two animal researchers from the National Institutes of Health, closely barbered and wearing somber suits with tasteful ties, were to face two members of The Mercy Bandits, an animal rights group wanted for several destructive acts in experimental laboratories across the country.

The Mercy Bandits were self-proclaimed terrorists. They had taken their name from a now-famous British organization, The Band of Mercy, founded in London in the waning years of the nineteenth century. A documentary celebrating the Band's good deeds still aired from time to time on public television. The Band of Mercy members, a group of well-to-do women, many of them wives of members of Parliament or captains of industry, set about rescuing emaciated cart horses from their drivers and nursed them back to health. Sometimes these rescues involved prodigious acts of heroism: women in hobbled skirts striking out with their umbrella tips against drivers armed with horsewhips, women throwing themselves onto overloaded wagons, hurling lumber and metal scraps into the street. Women secretly sequestering guineas from their domestic allowances in order to buy off indifferent owners of the beasts of burden. The authentic period costumes, the replicas of actual dray wagons and rude carts had won the program two citations for excellence.

Their bodies veiled behind screens, their voices altered so as to be unrecognizable, the talk show Mercy Bandits fidgeted in their easy chairs. They were, after all, fugitives from justice, a certain kind of justice untempered with mercy. Less well known than Greenpeace, they were equally flamboyant, seizing impounded dogs, cats and pigs, burning lab records, releasing hundreds of caged mice and birds. They had infiltrated and secretly filmed dozens of animal experiments, they had graphic footage of monkeys' heads being smashed, cats' forelegs broken, rabbits' eyelids sewn open, rats subjected to repeated electric shocks, all in the interests of science.

"Somebody has to do what we're doing," the large, squat shape declared. "Once people understand what's going on in these so-called scientific labs they'll band together, they'll put a halt to these sadistic procedures."

"Look," the younger of the two NIH representatives said. "Would you rather still have polio epidemics? If it weren't for Jonas Salk's experiments on monkeys, we'd still have wards full of paralyzed children, people in iron lungs and so on."

"Isn't that a good point?" Geraldine Huckaby spoke throatily into her microphone as she cruised the aisles for audience reaction. So far, it was about evenly divided between boos and applause. "Isn't that valid?"

But the agitated woman she chose to call on had a different agenda. "What about these cocaine experiments, why are you injecting infant monkeys with cocaine, then giving them electroshock tests? If you want to find out the behavioral effects, that's what you say you're doing, aren't there enough crack babies right here in Los Angeles? New York? Washington? Why not conduct your lifesaving experiments on human infants?"

"We're talking at cross-purposes here," said the older suitcoat-and-tie. "Look at antibiotics, look at smallpox vaccinations, look at how we've virtually eradicated measles in the US, all thanks to animal research, humanely conducted."

Geraldine had moved to the other side of the aisle; it was time to call on a man.

"I'm a third year med student at UCLA. Don't believe this...bull about humanely conducted. The only regulations in effect say how small a cage can be, say that there has to be food and water. Not that it can't be withheld, just that it has to be there. Researchers can do what they want with the animals they are experimenting on, they can withhold painkillers if they think painkillers will influence the results, they can cut, burn, freeze, force poisonous gases into their lungs, whatever suits their methodology, if you can call it that. Right now here in southern California there are two labs still running these redundant experiments on maternal separation anxiety. How many times do you have to take the primate mother away from her baby to prove that they both suffer? Are we deaf, dumb and blind to the implications? How many helpless infant monkeys have to be rendered catatonic to prove a point everyone in this room understands?"

A loud chorus of boos and cheers ensued. The two Mercy Bandits sat silent. Their work was being done for them.

"You may be in med school," said the older of the two NIH representatives, "but what you obviously don't understand is that there are critical measurements, critical endocrinological measurements still to be taken. The relationship between parental care, the neurobiology of touch and the chemistry of stress is providing us with new insights into how the brain of the newborn develops. We're looking at the production of key biochemicals that inhibit CRH, the master stress hormone...."

One of The Mercy Bandits seized her microphone. "That's a crock of you-know-what. What you're really saying is that there are millions of federal dollars to be had. All you need to do is think up a project that sounds interesting and you're likely to get funded. It's the novelty of the idea and your good connections that pay off. Meanwhile, billions of dollars are spread around, six million animals a year are exterminated, hundreds of young researchers are trained and sanctioned as sadists...."

The dialogue went unfinished. A series of stink bombs exploded in the audience and there was a collective gasp as sulphurous fumes permeated the enclosure. The room emptied as magically as in a Disney cartoon. Carla was extruded along with the rest. But driving back to Montandino she let herself review her heady conversion to The Mercy Bandits.

At the end of a *wanderjahre* after college— she had graduated from the Rhode Island School of Design with high honors and her parents had provided the capital for her European tour— she paused in London before flying home. On the bulletin board of the youth hostel she was staying in she saw a hand-lettered poster announcing an upcoming meeting of an unnamed animal rights organization.

"Who are they?" she asked a fellow hosteler.

"Oh, that's The Mercy Bandits," he told her. "Everybody knows who they are, they just don't say so. It's like, you know, the love that dares not speak its name?"

Everything British intrigued her, a clandestine poster especially. She decided to look in.

The somewhat seedy hotel conference room was packed with dedicated followers, people who wore only cotton or linen, who picketed butcher shops and furriers, who never touched flesh or eggs or milk products. Secret films taken in abbatoirs, experimental labs, poultry and veal calf barns were being shown continuously. A young couple who had been indicted four times for illegal actions spoke eloquently about how they had smuggled cameras into major medical laboratories to record animal abuses.

Volunteers were enlisted for a night mission to liberate a population of hamsters being used in a cosmetics laboratory, their backs shaved raw, to test the toxicity of a new line of foundation makeup. People — mostly older women — stood docilely in line to sign up for what was certain arrest. Their cause made perfect sense to Carla; it scratched her divine itch and changed her life.

V

IT WAS RACHEL BARANOFF'S idea to steal the squirrel monkey pair, the first of a new shipment, the ones that were due to be separated at the end of spring break. But it was Ben — Reuben, her twin — who made it feasible. Rachel hadn't been able to think past just snatching them out of the cage and leaping into Ben's newly restored VW bug, the one he'd worked on a whole year before he was old enough to register and drive it on the road.

Twins in general tend to take their mirrored selves for granted. The twin children of twins seem to identify with the other in a sort of geometric progression. What comes of sharing a playpen, of putting another's toes in your mouth may be genetically intensified. Rachel and Reuben grew up disliking the same foods — lima beans, for instance. Their sneezes were identical. When they read silently they frowned from time to time and touched the tips of their noses with their index fingers. And, unaware they were doing so, they finished each other's sentences.

Their father, Hal Baranoff, and their uncle, his twin brother Vance, were no longer speaking. Perhaps they were re-enacting their adolescent schism. But Hal's fraternal twins were as fiercely bonded as tribal aborigines.

Reuben was the practical one. "First of all, how're you gonna get the keys to break in Sunday night?"

"Easy, Greasy. I already stole them off Manuel's keyring last Saturday while he was cleaning cages. You know how he always hangs the whole big ring up on the hook by the door so none of the monks can grab it off him while he's working? Well, when I went in to talk to him — he's such a sweet man, he always lets me visit when he's the one on duty— I just waited till he was down the other end. And then I opened the whole chain and let the keys all fall to the floor so it'd look like he just didn't hang the ring up right. The door locks shut when you go out, you don't need a key for that."

"I wonder what he did the next time?"

"There's a master set in the office. By now he's probably had new ones made so Daddy won't find out and scream at him."

"All right," Ben said, considering. "So after you snatch the monks, where'll you keep them?"

"Don't know. Maybe Carla'd take them till we could figure it out."

"*Not*. They're so inquisitive, they'd tear her place apart in ten minutes, you know that. They need a secure place, out of the weather, an outdoor pen somewhere."

"I could ask Amanda to ask Luis out at the stables."

"Jesus, Ray! Everybody in southern California would know in ten minutes there were two stolen monkeys in a box stall."

"Well, Mr. Know-It-All, any ideas?"

"I was sort of thinking about Joanna Hammerling."

"Oh God, Benny, that would be wonderful! It's miles and miles from town and now you're working out there part-time and all. She has tons of room and barns...."

"What I was thinking was she has these dog runs with heated kennels from back when she used to breed Dobermans. And a couple of them are way out from the house, behind the llama shelters."

Joanna Hammerling was salty, reclusive, and very rich. She had inherited her grandfather-in-law's fortune, or what was left of it after he had endowed the Hammerling School of Engineering. She sculpted in metal, welding chunks of

rusted steel together to create improbable giraffes and el-
ephants, dinosaurs and alligators of fearsome proportions.
Ben loved to watch her wrestle some ragged six-foot strip
of metal into position with her thickly gloved left hand and
reach for the arc welder with her right. She would nod her
head downward so sharply that the protective visor slid
down over her face; as she touched her torch to the metal
the air would instantly turn acrid.

Although she had worked from live models for years cre-
ating respectable torsos and heads that, once cast in bronze,
were suited for indoor display, after old Hammerling
crumped (her words exactly), she had picked up the acety-
lene torch and taken off for local junkyards. It was she who
had helped Ben weld a new used floor into his VW Beetle
after the old one dropped out onto his father's driveway.
"There you go, Benny," she'd said. "It's in there now, tighter
than a virgin's cunt."

If his mother had been eavesdropping, Ben would have
blushed. He was, after all, her wholesome, intelligent, good
son. He was at the top of his eleventh grade class, making a
beeline for Harvard or Yale with his straight teeth and strong
tennis game. He planned to major in political science and
work in a soup kitchen on the weekends. Meanwhile, he
smoked pot with his buddies, rode into L.A. whenever he
could cadge a ride, and had just started screwing his girlfriend Marilyn, who was a track star and a cheerleader.
Together they studied articles in magazines like *Cosmopoli-
tan* that promised to teach "13 Ways to a Better Sex Life" or
"Multiple Orgasms: Myth or Reality?" He and his cheerful
freckled Marilyn wanted to get it right the first time. Usually they did it in the desert now that he had his own wheels
(he was still forbidden to drive to L.A., to his chagrin), but
once she snuck him into her house while her parents had
gone to theater in the city and they rolled around for hours

on the smooth sandfree sheets.

He hadn't told Rachel he was getting it on with Marilyn. In some cockeyed way it was a disloyalty to their twinship to be doing it. But it was even more disloyal not to tell her. He figured she knew by now anyhow, or if she didn't, she'd soon figure it out. Everyone says that girls grow up faster than boys but that wasn't how it was with the two of them. Ray wasn't ready for sex, he could see that. He wished he could talk to her about it; it was the first secret he could remember keeping from her since his brief venture into a secret society of eight-year-old boys who mostly held pissing contests behind the Baranoffs' three-car garage.

The twins drove out on Good Friday, after school, first south on 287, then east on 45, toward the desert. Something mysterious worked in you out here, Rachel thought, admiring the first cholla and ocotillo cactuses, the faint blooms enlivening the manzanita. To live on the verge of desert as Joanna Hammerling did was to be open at all times to the seam of horizon with its red rocks in one direction, its snowcapped peaks in the other. You were never taken by surprise; visitors were visible miles off.

Joanna agreed to the conspiracy. "But remember, if you get caught, I didn't know a thing about it. I never go that far back on the property because I'm terrified of rattlers." She gave Rachel a broad wink. Rachel couldn't believe there was anything short of a nuclear drop that terrified this woman.

"We'll bring their monkey chow," Rachel promised. "They love oranges and apples, and raisins and any kind of nut, if you want to give them treats. And I promise I'll drive out every single day to clean the kennel and look after them."

"In whose car, Smartass?"

"Yours." She stuck her tongue out at him fondly.

The thing about being twins was you were never alone.

You rarely argued because it was like fighting with yourself, which hurt, and you didn't keep anything back, either.
Though now she had a best girlfriend, Amanda, and they
were such pals and rode Amanda's parents' horses almost
every day after school, she and Ben were growing apart.
Well, not growing apart exactly, but moving sideways. He
had his own sort of clique of guys he palled around with.
The girls were all crazy about Ben and he frequently drove
around the village with two or three chosen ones at a time,
running errands or just cruising.

He and Marilyn were an item now. She didn't like to
think about it too much. It thrilled and scared her to picture them doing it; she supposed they must be doing it by
now, which was okay as long as they took precautions.
Benny, she was sure, would take precautions.

He hadn't shut Rachel out or anything, but it felt good to
be conspirators again. From the time they were toddlers
they'd joined forces against the adults; not just their parents, but all the grownups who oohed and ahed over them
for looking alike, for being the same and yet not the same,
as if they wanted it that way, or could help it.

Their father had gone camping in the canyon over Easter, something he did periodically to relieve the stress of his
job. Their mother had flown to San Francisco for her an-
nual visit with her only sister. The twins could have gone
with her. Ben of course was too old to go anywhere with a
parent unless it was a full-family do, a state occasion. Part
of Rachel had really wanted to. It would have meant shopping and ballet and fancy restaurants, but a bigger part of
her wanted to stay at Amanda's and get ready for the spring
schooling show. It was a three-phase; Rachel was going to
ride her first cross-country course at the prelim level.

In the olden days of course, Lottie would have stayed
with them. Lottie, who cleaned and babysat when they were

little and even sometimes cooked when their mother, Susie Hagedorn Baranoff, a columnist for the *California Gourmet Gazette*, had to be away. In her absence they had the forbidden treats that were Lottie's specialty: mayonnaise and sugar sandwiches on white bread, mashed potato sailboats swimming in cream gravy, and for dessert, vanilla ice cream smothered in a whole jar of maraschino cherries. They stayed up late with Lottie, who poured from, then dribbled water into, their father's scotch and snuggled them in her own bed with its distinctive sweet-stale smell.

Sometimes Lottie's grown son came to visit. Drew had been a cowboy and a trick rider. He knew everything about horses, especially the mean ones, the rogues, as he called them. Rachel was in awe of him but he scared her at the same time with his fierce expression and hard-heeled stride. Sometimes he stayed out on the desert at Joanna Hammerling's; sometimes he inhabited the Baranoff basement game room. Rachel was always relieved when he left town again to help out on the fall roundup, the spring branding, or just out of a restlessness that kept him from putting down roots anywhere. "He goes in and out like the Cheshire cat," Lottie said.

Lottie said twins were a gift from God. Lottie said twins would always stick together. Whenever Reuben and Rachel said something at the same time she taught them to hook their little fingers and recite: "What goes up the chimney?" "Smoke." "May your wish and my wish never be broke."

Now Rachel's wish was coming true.

◻

She and Ben struck at midnight. Rachel tiptoed out of Amanda's household of sleepers at 11:45 and met Ben on the corner, as they were both fearful his car's distinctive putt-putt might alert the family. Because he was a boy he was on a longer leash. He and his pals had gone to a vampire movie in Napara and afterwards he split, supposedly to drive back to the Hammerling ranch. Mrs. H. had allotted him the now-unused bunkhouse from the old days when Drew Deveraux tended her belted Galloway cattle, her Palomino horses, her prize llamas and Dobermans, before the twisted metals stage.

There wasn't another car on the street as they drew up to Graysmith. The building loomed on the landscape like some massive fortress; just the sight of it gave Rachel goosebumps. Ben eased the Bug into a slot behind the shrubbery. They both got out of the car without so much as clicking the doors closed.

Rachel's stolen key slipped easily into the lock. She turned it so softly yet dexterously that they could both hear the tumblers click. Their sneakered feet padded up the stairs. Another insertion of the metal tongue and they were in the monkey house. No lights, they'd agreed beforehand, not even a flashlight. Nothing to set the creatures off. The room was crepuscular yet familiar to Rachel. Most of the inhabitants were asleep on the floor of their cages, curled in fetal position in the back corners, but several rustled and got up as she and Ben tiptoed down the corridor.

Although the shaking of bars, the pounding, rattling and screeching of captive primates was commonplace, even beyond notice, it was vital, Rachel said, not to stir things up any more than necessary. She didn't say that the monkeys' standard daytime ruckus unnerved her, that she longed to demolish the cages, liberate all these desperate beings that her father held in durance vile. It was an expression she had only lately learned from her history teacher and it was apt.

And now she was at the squirrel monkey's cage and

reached in and made soft hoo-hooing noises she had learned from the monkey and proffered three raisins on her flattened palm, just as she had done every day last week when Manuel had let her visit, and her darling mother monkey plucked first one, then another. As she reached for the last one Rachel ever so gently lifted her with her baby tightly attached to her fur, and Reuben stepped from behind her and flung a terrycloth bath towel over the mother and baby in Rachel's arms and this time they clattered downstairs heedless of the racket, raced from the building and catapulted into the VW. The engine obediently turned over. They careened out of the driveway of the parking lot and sped halfway down the street before Reuben came back to his senses, slowed down and flicked the headlights on.

Rachel cooed and sang to the monkeys all the way out of Montandino. They were so soft and cuddly with expressive eyes and round noses the size of a chocolate dollar. She had to admit to herself that she probably wouldn't have had the courage to kidnap a macaque pair. They were a lot bigger and fiercer, with wicked incisors. Rachel had seen that they learned early; when humans came to take them out of their cages, it was to make them suffer.

One of her father's lab assistants had worked in a similar setup at Berkeley. He told her that there, after the macaques had bitten a couple of workers, they were tranquillized and the skin at their waists was stitched to make handles — love handles, he called them — so that when a person wearing elbow-length gloves reached into the cage he could grab one like a package and still be safe from its teeth. Rachel had had to resist putting her hands over her ears during this recitation. It was what she used to do when she was little and people forced truths upon her.

Joanna Hammerling had laid in an entire bale of straw for a bed and the squirrel monkey pair settled in quite calmly, the baby clinging to her mother's front but turning her head to look soulfully at Rachel.

They drove back to Montandino in silence. Rachel dared to rest her head on Benny's shoulder; she told herself she had never been happier. Ben amused her by whistling and humming *Humoresque* at the same time, a technique he had perfected in the sixth grade. When he turned down Amanda's street he cut the motor and headlights at the same time; Rachel slipped out the passenger side and closed the door as firmly as she dared. He held his breath as she tiptoed up the walk. It was 3 a.m.

Because she had left the front door unlocked it was no trick at all to slip back in. She hoped Ben hadn't dozed off on his second roundtrip back to the Hammerling place. At least they'd saved one pair of the new shipment. She couldn't bear to think of the others somewhere en route to the Graysmith torture chamber in their wooden crates, doomed to be separated one by one until they were driven crazy.

Since there was no way to stop him, she often lulled herself to sleep by fantasizing her father dead. She killed him off in an accident on the freeway, or in a plane crash, something swift and merciful. How simple life would be without Dr. Harold Baranoff in it! Even though she used to love him when she was a little girl and he was a confident laughing young father who rode her piggyback around the house, she really wished him dead.

VI

ON THE WEDNESDAY before Good Friday, Vance organized a little ecumenical Seder at his cottage. What the hell? Wasn't it all the same tradition? Since Easter had the calendrical good fortune to fall in the middle of Passover week this year, he, Vance Baranoff, would commemorate Jesus's Last Supper with one of his own.

Hal and his wife Susie and the twins came, as did Normie, an old pal of Vance's, a poet he had known back in grad school, who was now doing screenplays in L.A. He brought along his wife, who supplied the gefilte fish, and his two sons, who would help read the four questions. Digger came, too, with Theresa. Vance had first gotten to know Digger when he went to buy a license for his new dog, Arthur. It turned out that he and Digger shared an enthusiasm for fly fishing, something Digger lamented he had little time for. Vance allowed as how he hadn't fished a river since he'd come to Montandino but he was hoping to get up into the high country one of these weekends. Digger thought he knew just the right place to go in the Sierras, maybe the two of them could cut out one Monday or Tuesday— weekends were likely to be his busiest periods. Vance said that maybe the best thing— the only best thing— about being a writer was that you could keep flexible hours.

Digger then said that the best thing about being Chief was that you got to be married to Theresa. Without her, his office would be reduced to rubble. Theresa was used to this kind of public compliment; she merely smiled.

But Carla, whom Vance had known back East and who was now his neighbor in the Riva Foundation's art studio, begged off. She desperately needed the quiet time to finish a weaving that was going to the exhibit in Washington at the Renwick.

"Why is this night different from all other nights?" Rachel asked.

"On all other nights we eat all kinds of herbs. Why on this night do we eat especially bitter herbs?" Ben recited.

Normie's sons were encouraged to read the other questions and Vance provided an abbreviated version of the bondage-in-Egypt story from a Xerox of the newly revised Haggadah. He found he hated the new version. All the lyrical, archaic language he remembered from his boyhood had been leached out of it.

But Normie said, "'The poetry is in the pity.' That's from Wilfred Owen, you guys. The point is, we were all Pharoah's slaves in Egypt. We're all Jews in the Exodus together."

Although he had married out of the faith, Hal mistrusted any crossovers among religions. He had married a goy. And if he hadn't gotten her pregnant? *Dayenu,* it would have been enough, as the Seder responsive reading goes. He would have married her anyway. And if they hadn't lost that first baby? *Dayenu*; there might never have been the magical Reuben and Rachel. Susie never complained about her lost Episcopalian identity. She told him she'd gone to half a dozen Seders before she even met him; more Seders, for that matter, than Easter services.

Hal said it was tacky to be reading the service from Xeroxes, to say nothing of trespassing on the copyright. As for Seder and Purim with gefilte fish and poppyseed turnovers, as for Hanukah with potato latkes, as far as he was concerned, Judaism was strictly a kitchen religion these days. Here they were holding a Seder with only a handful of real Jews present. His very own children didn't count, according to Jewish law.

After the door was opened for Elijah and the meal proper began, Vance and Hal started wrangling as if they were teenagers again. First, they argued about their joint bar mitzvah. Hal was still smarting over his Haftorah assignment of thirty-five years ago. Vance's, he claimed, had been easy. His was virtually impossible, the passage was some murky thing out of Deuteronomy. He knew he had flubbed it, he could hear the rabbi and the cantor whispering and see them shaking their heads. But then, he implied, he'd made a far greater success out of his life than poor unmarried, unchosen, unsold Vance.

Vance countered with sharp remarks about not torturing monkeys. At least he hadn't drowned one last month, was what he'd said.

"That was an unfortunate accident."

"More like a murder," Vance came back.

"You can interpret it any way you want, you're the novelist. At least that's what you call yourself."

"And what do you call yourself? The Marquis de Sade of behavioral psychology?"

"Fuck you, brother," Hal said. "We're leaving. Susie, kids, come on, get your jackets."

"Hal, Hal, it's Passover! Don't be like that, darling." Susie, who had provided the roasted lamb and asparagus, tried to restore order. "Come and sit down, darling. We're all family tonight."

But he would not be soothed. "I'm going home. The rest of you can stay here all night."

Hal's exit cast only a brief pall. "Let him go," Vance said. "When he's in a mood like this, he needs to be alone."

The meal was excellent, conversation friendly and witty. It was still early when the Seder concluded with Vance conducting a group singing of "An Only Kid."

"I wonder how much a zuzim is," said Digger.

"Zuzim is a plural," Vance told him. "I don't know what the singular is. A zuza?"

"You know," Digger confided, "there's nothing like this, whaddyacall it, family singalong? in the Church. Hell, I was an altar boy, I went to Mass way back when you couldn't even swallow water after midnight, the whole thing was in Latin and fish on Fridays and it was a sin to set foot in a Protestant church, let alone a synagogue."

Theresa agreed. "It was like that for us, too. But the world is changing, Digger. Thank goodness, even the Church is changing."

Vance threw an arm over Digger's shoulder. "We've all changed."

Rachel and Reuben departed in Reuben's Beetle to hook up with some of their friends; it was school vacation week and a spontaneous party was forming.

"Be home by midnight," Susie warned.

"Oh, Mom!"

"Remember, nothing good happens after midnight." It was a standing joke, the very admonition Susie had heard and disregarded when she was their age.

After everyone had gone, she and Vance finished the ceremonial bottle of Sauterne. Vance then opened the one he had held in reserve. He sat on the couch with his arm around his sister-in-law and grieved. What he felt was a kind of Weltschmerz, an all-pervading sorrow. The loss of the Passovers of his youth, the loss of that family feeling. No matter how tinged with jealousies and spite, they had once been a cohesive family. *Ma nishtanah, Why is this night?* And his father would recite the ancient words, "For this the Lord God led us out of Egypt," and his mother would pass around the dish with the matzoh, the lamb shank, the roasted egg, the parsley and horseradish. Old customs die hard. Maybe it *was* just a kitchen religion. Vance, who believed in nothing beyond the void, who proclaimed early and often of life that you only get one trip through, was homesick for something more.

"A penny," Susie said.

"I was thinking how much I want you. How much I've missed you, how much I always have."

He drew her to him and she lifted her lips to his. The kiss at first was tentative; then her mouth opened under his. After a long moment, she said, into his neck, "I give up. I don't have any willpower left."

"To send me away?"

"I sent you away seventeen years ago. What a fool I was! I've done nothing but regret it."

"'But that was in another country,'" Vance murmured.

"'And besides, the wench is dead.' Well, it's true. That wench died a long time ago. I think I was just too young to know what to do. Half-cooked, terribly unsure."

"It wasn't just youth, Suse. It was your goddamn stubborn loyalty. I loved you for it then. And now."

She got up then and wordlessly began to take off her clothes. She walked over to the window overlooking the chaparral and opened one of the casements outward. It was a warm and hazy night. A sliver of moon glimmered on the metal lip of the window. Vance tore his body free of his shirt, trousers. There was a knot in one of his sneakers; as he worked to undo it he saw that his fingers were trembling.

Finally, he came up to her at the window and turned her toward him. "Can't you see," he said, fitting himself against her. "Can't you see we belong together?"

Afterward they lay naked on his platform bed. The moon had disappeared; blackness pressed against the glass.

"I have to go. The kids, I told the kids they had to be home by midnight."

"I'll drive you back," Vance said. "But the twins. Do you think they're his or mine?"

She didn't answer. She turned toward him and seized him fiercely, and then she cried silently, lying there against him. He was ashamed that he had asked.

VII

RICK ENSLIN, 6'4", 270 lbs., a doctoral candidate and former football player from the University of Michigan, was studying altruism in three- and four-year-olds. Five mornings a week at the Graysmith Lab's playschool and kindergarten, he monitored their behavior patterns, recorded on camera instances of generosity and compassion, empathy and pity. He also caught scenes of outrage, grief, tantrums and general mayhem.

In the weekly phone call home he had tried to explain to his father, who was Enslin Construction.

"You mean you sit there and write down what these little brats are saying to each other?"

"Mostly I tape it. That way I can play it back."

"Doesn't seem to me kids that age know what they're saying. It's all hit and snatch."

"Not all. Anyway, that's the point. A lot of it is nonverbal, movement, gesture. You know, body language."

There was a long pause. His father grunted. That too was nonverbal but expressive.

For forty years, the Lab School had offered fifty spaces to toddlers and preschoolers on a first-come, first-served basis irrespective of their parents' ability to pay tuition. An endowment picked up the tab for little ones whose families fell below the upper middle-income base of the local professionals who enrolled their babies at birth. Because of its ethnically and economically diverse spread, the school had long been an attractive resource for Ph.D. candidates in psychology and early childhood education.

On the whole, Rick observed, children were not that different from what he had learned so far about primates. Altruism in monkeys seemed directly linked to family structure, the clan; it was Darwinian, designed to preserve and conserve the species. But in young humans he felt that he caught from time to time something beyond the survival quid pro quo. For want of a better word he called it selflessness. Perhaps what he occasionally saw was a glimmering of the soul, though he knew better than to put that unprovable concept on paper. Still, in a few short months he had amassed an enormous amount of material which would, he was confident, lead to a lively and original thesis.

He'd only come into the program the first week in January. But he'd been living in Montandino for two years before that, holding down a clerical job over at the Hammerling and sniffing around the edges of the Graysmith Lab like a rat seeking entry through a basement crevice. He'd made friends with the boss of the work crew there, a tough little man named Drew Deveraux, who knew everybody in town and hadn't a good word for most of them, especially the Graysmith Director.

Drew was a loner and Rick was a loner, too, although not by choice. Drew was a drinker; he could get right down into it if he had a mind to. Rick was content with the buzz a couple of beers provided. Drew had one living relative, a mother, somewhere in L.A., Rick surmised. "A dipso and a whore," Drew had said, then amended, "Ah shit. She's not a bad old lady. Just too goddamn susceptible to men, you know? 'Specially men in bars."

They were both workingclass stiffs, they knew what it was to scrape by. A big night out was pizza or Chinese, and once, a round of miniature golf. But something about Drew made Rick uneasy. It wasn't his foul mouth — women were all cunts or whores — but the relish he took in grisly stories. A murder, a rape reported on the tv news or in the paper became an obsessive conversation piece.

◻

After getting his Master's in early childhood development at U Mich, Rick's savings had run out and he went to work for his father. True, he had learned a lot in that year and a half. He was good with tools; he could set forms, pour concrete, frame up, hang windows, do blue wall and roofing. He could follow a blueprint down to the nth. He had to admit the pay was good— the old man didn't stint his only son. But nothing pleased him. If Rick came down for breakfast five minutes later than his father, he was a lazy sonofabitch. If a board split while he was nailing it, he was a clumsy sonofabitch. He was a stupid sonofabitch who didn't scree the concrete enough, his corner post was an eighth of an inch out of plumb, and what asshole set these louvers upside down?

Once he had the money in pocket for a year's tuition, Rick split. He came to California to fulfill himself, attain the grail, a Ph.D. in behavioral psych, which would open the doors of academe. Once he'd earned the degree, Rick planned to return to the comfortable homogeneity of Decatur, Illinois, and try for a teaching job in the vicinity. He'd left a tentative girlfriend and an antique MG behind. The first in his family to go to college, his acceptance in the Graysmith program would put the dumb jock image, the football scholarship, and the split fingers and blackened thumbnails of the building trade well behind him. It was a long, hard wait, but he'd finally gained admittance.

And then there was his classmate Felicity, ah Felicity. Was he half in love with this little redheaded, toughminded flirt? Or was she a flirt at all with her gorgeous hair that flipped from side to side when she turned her head, her hips that swivelled sinuously as she preceded him in the parking lot on their way to the usual fastfood for an order of their shared secret sin, french fried onion rings? He thought she probably couldn't help it, any more than he could control feeling horny whenever she swam into view.

Felicity Shugrue's focus was the acquisition of language and reading skills in four- and five-year-olds. It was a fruitful field. Ever since the introduction of computers, the Lab School had utilized reading readiness programs that greatly enhanced the skills of those youngsters who were mature enough to sit still in front of the screen.

She was also studying kinesic communicational behavior in children, patterns of facial displays, and how certain features of nonlanguage are carried over into speech. In her first report she had arrayed Munch's "The Scream" alongside a video of a kindergartner unwilling to relinquish a toy truck. His anguished howls of No! exactly fitted the painting. She was awfully damned smart, Rick thought, and more than that, she was effective. She had all the savoir faire he lacked.

Fifi—a nickname she detested—and Rick frequently lunched together. Rick invariably brought two enormous sandwiches and bought a Coke to go with. Felicity was more likely to pack a yogurt and some veggie nibbles. As spring progressed, the weather, never harsh, grew more hospitable. The lab provided picnic tables under a luxuriant stand of cultivated liquid amber trees. Sometimes Drew Deveraux ambled over and sat down with them. Felicity didn't like his horning in, but Rick always made room.

It was only natural to share a couple of pizza dinners in town and drive out to the movies in Napara. Once while Rick and Felicity waited in line to buy tickets to a Hollywood preview, Drew appeared and asked outright if he could join them.

Afterwards, Felicity protested. "I just don't like him, he gives me the creeps."

"He's been through a lot," Rick told her. "Cancer. They took out half his intestine, he keeps saying he has less than a year to live. Anyway, I don't see what's wrong with being decent to him. He's never done you any harm."

"I don't like the way he looks at me."

"What way is that?"

"As if I'm coming between the two of you. As if he hates my guts."

"The guy's lonely," Rick said. "He's probably scared, too. He's in pain. You know what it's like always to be hurting?"

She didn't. And she didn't want to hear any more, either. They spent a halcyon day together out in the desert wandering among the Joshua trees. They hiked up Mt. Ryan, an easy hike for Felicity's slim frame, though she had to admit that negotiating the switchbacks was tricky toward the top. Rick sweated heavily making the ascent. His calf muscles kept cramping up on him. But it was worth it for the spectacular view out over the desert. Now that they were out of the smog belt, the sky was as blue as a kindergartner's painting.

When he tried to make out with her, Felicity stopped him cold.

"This is absolutely not going anywhere," she told him. "We are friends, period."

"I know, I know."

"Well, don't moan about it, you big ape."

"I can't help it if I get turned on every time I'm around you."

"Well, we can fix that with a little behavioral modification."

She made the rules. She was brusque but tender. He got either a hand job or a blow job about once a week; he wasn't even allowed to fondle her breasts while she was doing him. Still, it was better than nothing, marginally better.

"That Drew person would be glad to do this for you."

"That's a shitty thing to say."

"What are you, deaf, dumb and blind?"

Felicity, ah Felicity.

❑

Dr. Harold Baranoff's background in the development of territoriality and communication among infants and children made him a logical choice for director of both their theses. He had impeccable credentials: a text on body position, facial expression and verbal behavior; another on kinesics and communication; and yet another on gesture and environment.

Rick found him formidable. "The guy's got ice water in his veins, I swear," he said to Felicity.

But she only murmured noncommittally; she was not going to be drawn into a discussion of the Director's character.

"Must be a gender thing," Rick said. "The way you get along with him. He doesn't seem to give a damn about what I'm doing."

Hal Baranoff's detachment was real. He was moving into a new sphere of interest —primate communication.

"It's a direct outgrowth of my earlier work," he explained to a visiting member of the Board of Overseers. "With these experiments we can unlock the key between human communication and primate communication."

In his initial grant application he had stressed that studying the reaction to separation in infant monkeys would prove immensely useful in analyzing and treating separation anxiety in humans, even carry over to the study of how to evoke positive feelings between the schizophrenic child and his mother.

Other researchers before him had demonstrated that such animal grants were readily replicated. The feds seemed to love them, which would make Hal's research fundable year after year. Only lately had a note of unease been introduced, with the unwanted publicity surrounding his maternal deprivation experiments.

Something else was grating on him as well. Fifi and Rick tossing a softball back and forth on the Graysmith lawn at noon. The two of them going off to the desert for the day and coming back God knows how late. This business of picnics and movies.

Fifi had reassured him. "He's just a brother. A sweet, goodhearted brother."

They were lying naked on satin sheets Fifi had found in Bed and Bath, lying in a patch of late afternoon sunlight in her rented house twenty miles out in the valley. His car was down in the village getting serviced; Fifi would drive him back on the pretext of giving him a lift to pick it up.

"You're not fucking him."

"I am not fucking him." Her tone was even.

He believed her and he didn't believe her. He was fifty-one years old, at the top of his form professionally and physically and possibly sexually as well. He had an attractive wife, remarkable children, and a wildly obliging playmate who was also his graduate student. Would she do anything to jeopardize her position?

On the other hand, she had the goods on him, if she ever wanted to defame him. Still, her word against his.... Not that she ever would. But suppose she let something slip to this sweet big brother Enslin? It was too risky. He'd have to go.

"Rick, I'd like a chance to talk to you in my office," Hal said on Good Friday morning, overtaking him in the play yard.

"Sure. I just need to stash the camcorder. I'll be right in."

Something in the Director's tone forewarned him. He was about to get a dressing down for something, but what? Just because you're paranoid doesn't mean they're not out to get you, he told himself.

Even so, he was not at all prepared for what followed.

"I'll come to the point," Hal said. "Bad news. Now that I've pretty much switched over to primate investigation, I'm sorry, but I'm afraid I'm going to have to cut you loose."

Rick, who had been sitting in the chair across the desk from the Director, sprang to his feet. "Cut me loose? What the fuck does that mean?"

"It means just that. I can't direct your thesis here. I don't have any faith in it. As I suggested to you earlier, altruistic behavior is invariably motivated by baser concerns. It is simply superficial reciprocity, even, or maybe especially, in young children."

"But I'm analyzing the whole range of cognitive conscious motivations that may be at the root of children's positive actions! I can just about predict empathic responses…."

"I know, I know. You've read Piaget on resolving moral conflicts, you're setting up your own paradigms. But if I'm going to direct a thesis, I have to feel some connection to the subject. And frankly, Rick, I just can't get into yours. And what with my own work, I don't have the time to be attentive to it. So I'm going to have to cut you loose."

"But you thought it was a great idea when I came in January." He paced the width of the office, turned and came back to where the Director was tipped back in his swivel chair.

"Now, Rick," Hal said soothingly, looking up. He could feel the adrenaline of fear shoot to his groin; this giant could deck him with one punch. "Sometimes it takes that long to see where an idea is going. I've read through your outline, I've taken a close look at your video with commentary, and it just doesn't wash. I wish it did, believe me. This is just as painful for me as it is for you. The kindest thing I can do is to tell you to pack it in."

"Pack it in." He was dumbstruck. Why, you lying, conniving sonofabitch, he thought. Just as painful. We both know why you're cashiering me. Better keep it in, don't lose your cool.

"What the hell am I supposed to do now?"

"My advice would be to start over elsewhere. This topic is dead in the water. If you want to stay in the area of early childhood, try to find a subject with some meat on it." He smiled ruefully.

More meat, hell, Rick thought. This isn't about my dissertation. It's about my having lunch with Fifi, our going to the movies together. Christ! She's probably told him she's my service station. No, she couldn't, she wouldn't, it would totally screw her program.

"Whereas Felicity's project is promising, right?"

"Remember, Felicity's been here since September, she's a lot farther along. And yes, her premise *is* promising. I feel it may eventually bridge the gap between human and primate vocalizations."

Fucker, Rick said to himself. "About my file. Will there be a letter of recommendation?"

"I don't see why not," said the Director. He exhaled with relief.

VIII

IT WAS A BEAUTIFUL DAY, the kind that back east might have been called a weather breeder, cloudless, with a sky so blue it suggested a ceiling done all in cobalt by a Renaissance painter. Felicity shut down her Power Book, restacked her notes and stripped for a long hot shower.

In truth, she would rather have been heading to Las Vegas to The Golden Nugget or The Flamingo. Hal had promised to take her gambling some weekend this spring but he had too much hanging over him right now. He said he needed to get into the mountains, breathe smogfree air, stretch his muscles. And unsaid, make love.

He was still a handsome man with the body of an athlete and the fresh aroma of expensive aftershave splashed freely about his face and neck. She loved fucking a man who smelled good, who sweated a clear animal sweat when he exerted. Someday they would ski together, or sail. Hal had hinted there was a cruise they might take. Even, next year, a field trip to South America if he could swing it, a grant to study maternal bonding in titi monkeys, little fluff-headed creatures that entered into monogamous relationships and kept strong family ties.

"You understand what would happen to both of us if word ever got out," he said to her the first time they came together.

"Of course I do!"

"I might be forgiven, eventually. Randy old men, after all, it's expected. But you'd be seen as having… fucked your way to a doctorate. Ouch!"

She dug her nails deeper into his buttocks. "You bad boy!

I'll have to teach you how to talk to your own candidate."

"But you admit you have the most to lose."

"More," she said. "Two people. A simple comparative."
She admitted nothing of the sort.

She massaged her face with sunscreen, tied back her
mane of hair and confronted her closet. Hal had warned it
might be cold up there, so she packed long johns and mit-
tens in her backpack. Toilet articles and sex toys went in
the outside zipper pockets. She tied her parka sleeves to the
straps, then hefted the bundle. Not too heavy; she'd be able
to reach the cabin easily before dark.

There wasn't a soul on the parking strip when she arrived, so Felicity angled the little red Honda behind some
shrubbery, not so much to screen it from later comers as to
keep it out of harm's way. She stripped down to her halter
top as she headed up the gritty trail into the canyon. In less
than a quarter of a mile, though, she was glad to pull her tee
shirt back on. The air was sharply cooler along the riparian
woodland stream. Sycamores and bay laurels grew in abun-
dance, punctuated here and there by a sentinel Douglas fir.

This early in spring the year-round brook roared rather
than sang. Water poured down dozens of rocky drops cre-
ating rapids and noisy eddies. If there were other hikers
this Good Friday noon, Felicity could not have heard them
over the stream's tumult. In places the trail closely paral-
leled the stream; higher up, it veered away to make room
for a series of rocky switchbacks.

By the time she had reached the first elevation marker
she was really sweating. It was a gratifying all-over sweat,
like a body lotion, and a faint breeze cooled her skin as she
walked. The canyon still scared her a little, the way the oaks
and alders closed in overhead in the lower reaches, the slip
and scrabble of decomposed granite underfoot, an occasional
mule deer startling out of the underbrush. A canyon wren

scurried and scratched in the leaves, then flew up to a nearby branch. They were rare enough that Felicity was pleased to have caught sight of one.

You didn't climb toward the wilderness boundary lightly. You came with proper gear, a water bottle and a clever knife, layers of clothes to warm you, raisins and nuts for the trail. Hal had taught her well. He adored the challenge, hurling his robust body against the walls of hills that rose up into mountains, marching steadily up as the trail narrowed, staying back from the tendrils of poison oak that blanketed the sides.

Hall especially loved to climb: climb, as opposed to hike. Once when they drove out to the desert at Joshua Tree, he carried the approved ropes, pitons, the mini-axe for carving hand and footholds. She watched enthralled as he climbed a rock face. He did it as methodically as if he were recording data, each move carefully calculated, a rhythmic vertical crawl up and over the torso, over the hip bone, inching across the breast, toeing hard into the rock nipple, up the knife of the clavicle, up and over the headless form of granite until he sprawled triumphant across the top.

For an East Coast agoraphobe she thought she was handling these rock-jock and peak-bagging things pretty well. She was street smart, knew how to stay away from doorways and alcoves when walking at night in the city. She carried her key ring between her second and third fingers, key tips pointing out, thumb clamped over the rabbit's foot. She knew how to go for the groin with the point of her umbrella; lacking all other resources, for the eyes with her fingernails. Self-defense and the willingness to scream were minimal skills for a woman alone in the city.

But the landscape here held other threats, the terrain was not necessarily benign. Snakes, spiders, rabid foxes, all possible, if not very likely. People talked about bobcats, though

Hal said he had never seen one. When sudden rains came in the desert, you could be swept away in a sudden torrent. She had seen the streets of Montandino fill up, float trashcans and vending machines off their moorings during a December downpour. Gorges previously cut by storms were awash in minutes. Anything caught there either drowned or was carried off, dizzied and dashed against the sides of the gully.

There were a dozen cabins grandfathered in the midsection of the canyon, from a time before the entire mountain was taken by the government and made into a national preserve. Felicity marvelled at the ingenuity and determination that had gone into their construction. Everything had to be hauled up the canyon by man or pack horse; every board, every bag of cement, every messkit and mattress. Some cabins sat on foundations of boulders prised from their original locations on the mountain. Others were raised on concrete pilings. There were decks and verandahs, toolsheds and outhouses, even a picket fence or two.

There had been more cabins, before the forest fire of '89 swept down from Arden's Ridge. The fire was eclectic, sparing some and devouring other dwellings, twice crossing the stream before it died away. Bereft owners were not permitted to rebuild; eventually, these eccentrically perched little chalets would rot away and be reabsorbed by the woodland. But Hal, who had charmed the octogenarian with his ability to read Hebrew, had the use of a lovely little two-room cottage that belonged to a retired professor of Semitic languages at Maartens Theological School.

Very occasionally Hal took his kids along for a weekend. His wife Susie chose not to make the climb. She said that weekends in the canyon were simply an exchange of sinks and she preferred her in-town modern one over the tin wash-tub on the mountain. Felicity could see some justice in that.

Susie and Hal were both Easterners, too. Almost every-body she had met in Montandino had roots in New Jersey or Maryland, Connecticut or New York. People out here said wryly that California was tilting into the sea from the weight of all the in-migrants. Carla, who conducted the weaving class Felicity had recently signed up for, was an-other East Coast native. In a way, Montandino was just a little hick town dotted here and there with flamboyant ec-centrics. No bar, no disco, not even a bowling alley. Felicity had hoped to find some other fun-loving younger women at the Riva Foundation studio, but she had soon been dis-abused of that notion. Carla herself seemed ageless, self-contained, even pretty in an understated way. She didn't invite confidences; speaking distance was as close as you got. She would never, Felicity thought, be a hugger.

At the 5,000 foot marker she took a break to munch on some trail mix and enjoy a long drink from her water bottle. Her body felt grateful for the rest, yet flexible and willing to take on the last thousand-foot stretch. To say nothing of the sexual athletics ahead.

Felicity was a realist about sex. It was an animal plea-sure, not to be ranked on the scale of such aesthetic delights as music or art or even the gustatory enjoyment of a fine meal. Animal pleasures were demands to be met, then set aside. Controlled, they were useful ploys a woman could use as stepping stones.

Long ago in high school in New Haven she had had a boyfriend, a football star a year older than she was. In the backseat of his Plymouth with the motor running and the heater going full blast— it was the coldest winter of the decade— he had inducted her into the academy of sexual pleasure. She remembered him fondly as a sweet and slav-ishly attentive boy. He reminded her of Rick. But then he went away to Reed and gradually they lost touch. A year later she entered Yale on a generous scholarship, one that bested offers from Smith and Wesleyan. Determined to carve out a career for herself, she set her sights on earning top grades. Everything else was secondary.

By the time she graduated from Yale University, Felicity had had a handful of casual relationships. She learned how to enter into an affair with contained enthusiasm and how to let go with minimal regret. The more you gave the more greedily men partook. The more you withheld the greater your leverage.

Her senior year she had met Kamal, gorgeous, swarthy Kamal, who was in the States on a fellowship exchange. His fierce eyes and bright teeth had dazzled her in the seminar on Freud, Jung, Adler and Klein, the Dialectics of Psychoanalysis. After six weeks they moved in together, each of them knowing it was a temporary arrangement.

Kamal provided her with a Ph.D. in the drama of fucking. She played every role from terrified virgin to wicked temptress, cruel stepmother to poor little matchgirl. And he went from king of the jungle to timorous Peter Rabbit, from wifebeater to abused child, moviestar hero to villain. He could play warrior, fag, or gangling adolescent with equal enthusiasm.

If she had earned her Ph.D. living with Kamal, Hal was providing her post-doc. Of course she had explored S & M with her young Turk, but Dr. Harold Baranoff raised it to new heights. They were kindred souls, sharing their sex toys like toddlers in a sandbox. She brought along the handcuffs, the nurse's uniform, enema syringe, KY jelly, the antique butter paddle she had found in a junk shop in Napara— she'd had to buy the pair. Hal had the amytal nitrite ampules and the Dior scarf he liked to use for prolonging climax.

Felicity understood that passion within marriage suffers

from the law of diminishing returns. It was up to her to keep this indoor sport surprising, sleazy and dangerous. Afterwards in her spacious valley house, naked and exhausted, they warmed up the Chinese takeout he had thoughtfully brought.

The house was a bargain rental from an academic couple now in Ireland on sabbatical. The doorbell played the first three notes of Beethoven's Ninth Symphony— or at least it had when Felicity first moved in. It didn't work at all now; Rick had said he would take a look at the wiring for her. He thought he could fix it, not that anybody came to call unexpectedly.

In return for the luxuries of musical doorbell and infrared heating lamp in the bathroom ceiling, Felicity looked after the two Persian cats who were declawed and could never go outside, pampered playthings of the childless medieval specialists. Named Elizabeth and Robert— after the Brownings, Felicity deduced— they were spayed and neutered littermates. Twins of another species.

Sometimes she and Hal met by prearrangement in one of those anonymous motels just off the freeway. He wouldn't take her to San Francisco or L.A., 29 Palms or San Diego; he was mortally afraid of being discovered. But she thought some of the thrill for him was in the tawdry nature of the affair. It was a textbook fact that famous men like to be disempowered sexually. To be spanked in a Super 6, to be threatened with an enema as she stood over him in her white nurse's outfit was one thing. To register at the Mark Hopkins or the Chateau Marmont would have legitimized the relationship and eaten away at its randy fabric.

It was getting dark once she had arrayed everything in the cabin to her satisfaction. There was a decent supply of wood and a cupboard stocked with emergency supplies of matches, candles, and several bottles of water. Lots of cans of gourmet foods, including artichoke hearts, caviar, and oysters. She started a fire in the fieldstone fireplace on the first try.

She wondered what Hal was carrying in his backpack. He bragged that he could tote 40 lbs. without strain and she believed him. Although he had hoped to start out by 3, he must have been waylaid at the last minute by a student. She was sure he'd be along soon and stood in the doorway looking down the trail she had mounted, willing the stillness to be broken by a moving shape. When she could no longer differentiate outlines in the gathering gloom she went indoors but did not turn the latch. She lit three candles and took out a packet of wild rice and chicken mix. She was ravenous.

IX

VANCE DROPPED OUT at the end of his freshman year at Bard College. It was a time for dropping out, tuning in to unheard melodies. Ironically, Hal had become the family's scholar, faithfully attending classes at Columbia and writing learned papers in abnormal psychology. Vance saw himself as part of a tradition of failure stretching back to the excesses of famous American writers, all the way back to Hart Crane, who jumped overboard to end his life.

He wondered if he might also be suicidal. Wandering through the peaks and troughs of his feelings, he poured out his angst into a journal which became a novel. *Here Today*, the coming of age of a sensitive boy suffocated by family and Old World mores, was hailed for its boldness and humor. "An excruciatingly honest new voice," Bell called him in *The New York Times*. "Hilarious and heartbreaking," said *Book World*. Vance Elias Baranoff, the twenty-two-year-old author of a best seller, dimpled behind his beard. He flew off to Marseilles, Majorca, Morocco with his fists full of travelers' checks.

While Hal Baranoff plodded through four years of the humanities and social sciences, Van Baran, as he was now known on his book covers, became a rover. *The Brand of Ishamel*, his second novel, was not so enthusiastically received, but the critics were tolerant. After all, second novels were notoriously difficult. A writer who faltered here might well be spurred to do his best work thereafter.

In truth, Vance felt squeezed by the competition. New voices were crying out of the Vietnam War from which he had absented himself. Napalm, torture, guilt, fragmented and passionate love stories, suicide, mass murder— how could he match the enormity of these enlarged-upon truths?

Meanwhile, Hal told him he had set his sights on a tenured position at the Graysmith Behavioral Sciences Laboratory in southern California. His groundbreaking work with young children had led to a textbook that was now frequently assigned in early childhood development classes. One of these days, he confided to Vance, once he was well installed and safely tenured, there might be grant money and time to pursue his hunches about the effects of maternal deprivation.

Meanwhile, a complication had arisen. Susie Hagedorn, a cuisine artist with her own catering business, was pregnant with his child.

"Do you love her?"

Of course he loved her. They were getting married upstate by a justice of the peace. Would Vance come along and stand up for his twin?

Vance rented a car and tailed them all the way to Rhinebeck. Nine months later, that baby was dead.

Susie was a long time getting over it.

"She's clinically depressed," Hal told his brother. "It's a classic postpartum. Disturbed sleep pattern, loss of appetite. Cries easily."

"God. You sound like a textbook, not a husband."

"We're doing the best we can. We've tried tranquillizers, mood elevators. Her doctor thinks a series of shock treatments...."

"That's a terrible idea."

Hal bristled. "You got a better one?"

Vance didn't answer. Sometimes he came up from the Village while Hal was teaching and cajoled her into going for a walk or to a movie. Sometimes they just sat for long stretches in the living room without speaking, listening to easy jazz music.

To his regret, he was falling in love with her. One night when some old friends had dropped by, Hal asked Susie to see what she could rustle up for a cold supper. He had gone out for deli to fill in.

Vance came into the kitchen to help; Susie, with her back to him, was rooting around in the fridge. Vance encircled her, gently letting his body lie against hers. She turned around and fitted herself against him. They kissed and he ran his hands down the sides of her breasts and held her close. But then there were footsteps and voices and she turned back to the refrigerator and started handing out salad greens to him, and a big jar of pickled herring.

The next day he persuaded Susie to take the subway down to the Village. It would be good for her, he'd said, she hadn't been out of the apartment in weeks. They would have lunch at this little bistro he frequented, and then take in an art gallery or two.

In his apartment he caressed the back of her neck, ran his fingers down her spine.

"Suse. Don't let them do the electroshock."

"Hal says it's the only thing that works in these cases."

"What cases? You're a person, not a case."

"You know. Postpartum.... But I'm scared."

"Hal's full of shit," he said, running his fingers through her hair, smoothing it back from her forehead, his mouth on her mouth, both sweet from the split of chardonnay at lunch, his tongue exploring the taste they had shared. He ran his hands over her breasts, feeling the nipples awaken under his touch.

"Please," she murmured.

"Please stop?"

But she turned to him on the sofa and shyly fumbled at his shirt buttons. He would never forget how they undressed each other, making it a delicate balancing act: her blouse, his shirt; her skirt, his jeans. She arched her back for him to undo her bra, he guided her hand inside his jockey shorts. They eased off the sofa to lie naked on the colorful Indian rug, stroking and nibbling.

"Oh God, Susie. I've wanted you for so long."

"Shh," she said. "Just hold me."

He pulled her on top of him and for a long moment she simply lay there, a welcome weight pressed against his entire length. Finally she straddled him and guided him in and together they surged forward in an ascending rhythm until she came first with a bird cry and he then followed, stunned with agonizing pleasure.

It was wonderful how Susie's depression began to lift. Her psychiatrist found it unremarkable. He called it spontaneous remission, not uncommon in such cases as hormonal balance was gradually restored.

Hal was gratified to have his woman back, as he put it. True, she couldn't seem to achieve orgasm, but that too would heal itself, he was confident.

The deception was terribly difficult for Susie.

"I never was any good as a liar," she said to Vance as they sprawled naked in a patch of sunlight on his bed. "We can't keep on like this."

"Leave him, Susie, leave him and come away with me."

◻

The herring became a talisman for Vance. He could never walk past jars of pickled herring in a supermarket without longing for Susie, who had, she finally told him, married the wrong brother. But she wouldn't consider leaving Hal. He needed her, she said. She didn't believe in quick divorces, she owed her allegiance to Hal, whose child she had carried.

"It's pride, isn't it?" Vance asked. "You have a perverse sort of pride in your staying power, sticking by your man."

"I just can't do it," she wept. Unspoken was her fear that he would go ballistic if she deserted him in favor of his twin. It wasn't a matter of her pride at all, but of Hal's. In a murderous rage Hal might very well track Vance down and kill him.

Somehow, they went on with their parallel lives. Vance had sublet his Village apartment and gone first to Paris, then back to Morocco, which suited him with its souks and secret alleys, its mayhem and passion. But eventually he came back to the States. Now on a book tour for his third novel, he chose to stay at the Chelsea. Susie dared to visit him once, then a second time that week. Even though more than four years had passed, they came together with the same urgency. Although she had sworn she would give him up forever, she came to his room for the last time on a rainy Sunday afternoon while Hal, at the top of his form, was giving a lecture at Princeton.

They coupled extravagantly, slowly, lingeringly. It was excruciating, having him and not having him. She was determined not to let him see her cry as she left his room on the fifteenth floor. It was the fifth anniversary of Angela's death.

❐

Susie thought she would never conceive again. But after a five-year hiatus, she carried twins to term.

X

THE LAB CLOSED at noon on Good Friday to allow employees an early getaway for the Easter break. All experiments were suspended for the week. The monkeys were back in their cages, seven rhesus macaque mothers and their offspring and one newly arrived squirrel monkey and baby, adequately watered and fed, and a rotating trio of graduate students was assigned to look after them until Manuel came in on Monday morning.

Students and staff alike scattered onto the freeways at the start of every vacation, desperate to escape the gridlock that was sure to overtake the road by the evening rush hour. Susie Baranoff had a 2 p.m. flight to San Francisco. She always looked forward to visiting Liz, her younger sister, now recast as somehow older and wiser. Liz was the owner of a popular boutique on Chestnut Street, just down the hill from the condo she and Warren had bought years ago, before the real estate market took off. Since then, it had soared out of sight; their paper profit was enormous. Of course, taxes had risen proportionately. And insurance, she was sure to explain earnestly.

Susie thought of herself by comparison as the country mouse. Even though she wrote a regular monthly column on culinary exotica for the *Gourmet Gazette*, even though she crisscrossed the state and forayed up and down the West Coast in search of new ways to prepare geoducks and prickly pears, her sister made Susie feel unworldly, especially in the chic department. Liz would fuss over her clothes, dress her in totally inappropriate pajama-like pant suits, swathe her in silk scarves and lacy lingerie. It was heaven to be pampered once a year. Easter was their time together. Christmas was bedlam in the boutique and over New Year's Warren and Liz always went up to Tahoe with two other couples to ski.

Tonight they planned to savor dinner at Chez Panisse in Berkeley. Tomorrow they had tickets for "The Phantom of the Opera," but before that, Susie was scheduled for a really good haircut at that Japanese salon Liz frequented. On Sunday, after Easter brunch and a stroll around the Marina, Liz had organized a sail around the harbor on a friend's forty-footer. There was a string quartet rehearsal on Monday. Tuesday, early, Susie would fly home. Four days of total freedom from the burden of being Dr. Harold Baranoff's life partner.

Four days free from the corrosive guilt of resuming her affair with Vance. She had let it happen, she had wanted it to happen. Hal's little tantrum at Vance's Seder was simply the catalyst. But what would happen next? What would happen to the kids if the stable family unit dissolved?

She thought she was probably using the twins as a screen to avoid facing the messiness of a divorce. After all, they weren't really children any more. Rachel was staying at her best friend Amanda's house, and Reuben was enjoying his new status as general factotum at Joanna Hammerling's ranch.

Susie supposed the kids were old enough at sixteen to leave alone in the house, but that prospect suggested beer parties out of control or worse. Marijuana at least; cocaine quite possibly. Not the twins so much as some of their friends. Not even friends; school buddies, peers. Peer pressure was like blood pressure. It rose under stress.

Thank God for Amanda's horses. Thank God for rich friends who owned not one, but two Thoroughbreds, the second one a skin-and-bones rescue two years ago, headed for the killers. Amanda was not only happy to share this largess with Rachel but depended on her for companionship on the trail, over fences and overnight. When they weren't physically together, Susie reflected, the two girls were connected by the umbilicus of the telephone.

Amanda's second horse, snatched from the knacker with Rachel's connivance and their combined suit of both sets of parents, had proved to be a sweet tempered, modestly talented hack. Rachel, who half-leased him, named him Practical Magic because, she said, "It was practically magic that we got him." The girls called him Madge. Reuben called him Mr. Madge lest he be mistaken for a mare. Hal called him that damned horse but paid their share of the monthly board bill without comment. Susie, to whom horses were as alien as bison, had come to enjoy Magic. She stood at the end of the lead shank while Rachel finished the final grooming. After Rachel mounted, she took the polishing cloth and swiped the toes of her boots clean, then blew a kiss as her heroic child trotted sedately off to the show ring.

As for Hal, she could see that he was increasingly depressed by the bad publicity his monkey research was raising around town. There had been a piece in the local *Clarion* followed by a writeup of a fracas at the Huckaby talk show, where Hal's project had been mentioned. She cheered inwardly to think that public opinion might shut the lab project down.

Whenever she dared let herself, she enlarged a fantasy of life without Hal. A simple, reduced-to-daily-essentials-life somewhere far from Montandino, some medium-sized town in a flyover state, say Kansas or Nebraska, where in blessed anonymity she was no longer the Director's wife. Perhaps Rachel would bring Magic with her to this new life much as Reuben would bring his restored VW. They could finish high school in her mythical Prairie Town, win scholarships to eastern establishment universities, and Susie could grow old gracefully, listening to NPR, humming at her loom, and indulging her taste for curries and spicy salsas.

Ever since meeting Carla she'd entertained this notion of independence, of a new destiny. There was that famous Thurber cartoon, "When did the magic go out of our marriage?" Once she and Hal had been desperately, romantically in love. Courting her, Hal had been a considerate, even tender, lover. That first year of the pinchpenny graduate school life, the grind of papers to write, exams to prepare for, seemed to enhance their pleasure in each other even as her belly swelled. Angela's death was a turning point.

Should she blame herself for grieving overlong? Was it her fault that years passed before she could conceive again? All that loveless fucking with calendars and temperature charts and the dreadful office visits, and then finally the miracle of twins. They still had a sex life of sorts, but Susie found herself repelled by Hal's penchant for experimentation.

That morning Hal had said he was going up to the cabin alone for a few days of R & R. Maybe yes, maybe no. She knew he was a rover. She could tick off two former students she suspected he had conducted affairs with in the past. It seemed likely there was a new one in the present.

It was a relief, really. His tastes had grown increasingly kinky. She didn't know what it was — midlife crisis? Male menopause? She wished she could be as serene as Carla. Carla gave off an aura of quiet competence. Susie felt frazzled most of the time.

En route to the airport she thought back to that dark day last February when she was the only member of Carla's weaving class to make it to the Ravi Foundation. Sheets of wind-driven rain had swept sideways over the chaparral and scattered a newly planted stand of palm trees like so many pick-up sticks. Umbrellas turned inside out. As they invariably did during downpours, the streets of Montandino filled with water, and the town's maintenance crews brought out of storage the traditional wooden walkways that enabled pedestrians to cross at major intersections without submersing up to their ankles.

Susie had left her car at the bottom of the hill and arrived on foot, soaked through, uncertain what had impelled her to make this trek. Still, it was class day; was she just being dutiful?

"Goodness," said Carla. "Aren't you the brave soul."

Susie thought that Carla wasn't thrilled to see her. She had probably been looking forward to a quiet stretch alone.

"Here, come on back, let me lend you some dry things." In her bedroom Carla rummaged through some drawers and handed Susie a jogging suit. "How about some slippers? Let me have these"— she gestured toward Susie's soggy jeans and turtleneck — "and I'll toss them in the dryer."

As she trailed Carla into her bedroom, Susie noticed a triptych of snapshots on the bureau in a Lucite frame. They were all seemingly taken on the same bright fall day. A tall slender man with a strictly trimmed beard was tousling a large dog in the lefthand photo. In the middle, he sat spraddle-legged, his back against a willow, and grinned into the camera. The righthand snapshot had caught him and Carla together in a sober moment. It was an awkward pose, given their difference in height, but the overall effect was charming. Arms around each other's waists, shoulders back, chins high, they both looked off into the distance as if awaiting marching orders.

Susie said as much.

"We were," Carla said. "We left that same day for a Greenpeace demonstration."

"Where is he now?"

"Dead."

"Oh, God," Susie said.

"Killed three years ago in a stupid traffic accident in up-state New York."

Susie winced and shook her head as if to deny it.

"He was hit head on by a drunken driver with a sus-pended license."

"I'm sorry. I didn't mean to...."

"It's all right, how could you know?"

"He's so...," Susie searched for a word. "Comely. You know. What was his name?"

"Marc Brownstein. We were partners for ten years."

"Partners?"

"Lovers. Unmarried, by choice. Does that surprise you?"

"Not in the least," Susie said, rallying. "He looks...ter-rific. I mean, full of energy."

"Ardent. Committed," Carla amended. "Also, lots of fun."

It surprised Susie how comfortable she felt in Carla's private space. Wouldn't she ordinarily have taken the dry clothes off to the bathroom and changed there? Instead, she stood in the middle of the room and shucked her wet things, briefly toweled her damp thighs with the terrycloth Carla wordlessly held out to her, and proceeded to pull on the jogging suit.

"You know, we lost a child once," she told Carla.

"Really?"

"Years and years ago, long before the twins. Hal was still at Columbia, SIDS, if you know what that is, sudden infant death syndrome, a name doctors attach to it when they have no other explanation."

"It must have been terrible for you."

"The worst was how I kept blaming myself. Like if I'd only been there, I could have saved her."

"I think people always think that."

"My o.b. insisted it was a natural phenomenon, nature's way of purging incomplete or deficient newborns."

"That's a big help." Here, Carla turned and led the way into the studio. She flicked on the bank of fluorescent lights overhead.

"I know. I said, if that's true, then why the Downs children, why all the cystic fibrosis, why the babies born with one arm or fish flippers or only a brain stem and no brain? Why *my* baby? She was perfect in every respect."

"My mother used to tell me over and over, Life is routinely unfair."

"She was eight weeks old," Susie said. "I'd pumped breast milk for her, I had to be out of town just overnight for the magazine, I was writing for *Food Thoughts*, a kind of East Coast version of the *Gourmet Gazette*. Boston, I could get back in two hours, two hours! Hal urged me to go, he said I was turning into one of those over-possessive mothers and didn't I trust him to take care of his own child, for God's sake."

"So you went."

"So I went and before I came back she was dead. He said she slept past her feeding and when he went in to check on her she had simply stopped breathing. Simply."

Carla murmured and shook her head.

"I couldn't stop thinking he'd done it. I went to a psychiatrist three times a week for almost a year."

"And that helped?"

"I finally stopped letting myself think it."

"What willpower."

"Otherwise they were going to try electroshock."

The two women looked at each other for a long moment. Finally Carla said, "Sometimes an obsession is an earned thing."

"Maybe he didn't do it. Probably he didn't do it. But the

thing is, he could have. He was capable of doing it. I read an article that said forty percent of sudden infant crib deaths are caused by one or the other distraught parent."

"Was he distraught?"

"Hal can't stand crying babies. He can't stand the sight of blood. Once, he had an infected finger, it had to be lanced. He'd driven a splinter under the nail and eventually it festered. When the surgeon just sliced it open in his office, Hal turned green and fainted dead away."

But he wasn't a monster, Susie told herself, pulling into the airport Park 'n Fly. He was a generous and loving father, he had been a pillar of strength to his own parents, the very model of a devoted son. He had flown east every other weekend the entire year that his father was dying. Even when his mind went Hal treated him with dignity and tenderness and when the coffin was lowered into the soggy earth of Long Island, Hal had seized a shovel and insisted on helping to bury the body.

When Lottie, who had looked after the twins from the first year they had come to California, when warm, loving, alcohol-befuddled Lottie had fallen apart in their living room, it was Hal who had arranged for her entry into the Open Door detox. It was Hal who paid the huge monthly bill.

Truly, truly he had tried to save their beloved Lottie. He even managed to be civil to her son, who had a positive talent for arriving on the scene in midcrisis. Drew, who hated women, Eves, all of them, Drew, who adored his mother as much as he despised her. Even though Hal could be harsh and demanding to his subordinates, he handled Drew's outbursts with sympathy and tact. And therefore he didn't kill Angela, she told herself firmly. Or if he did kill her, it was by neglect, not on purpose. Because if he did kill her, she could kill him.

XI

HAROLD BARANOFF was intercepted by his brother just outside his office at 3 p.m. Vance had been lurking in the building for some time, out of sight first in the men's room, then behind the door of an adjacent office, watching for the place to empty out.

"Hey bro, how's it going?"

Hal was immediately suspicious. They were no longer on congenial terms since the publication of the Clarion article and the blowup at Vance's Seder. "What're you doing around here?"

"Waiting for you. I've got something I want to show you."

"Well, make it snappy. I don't have much time."

They fell into step together and came out the back entrance onto the parking lot.

"It's over here, in my car."

"That's not your car," Hal said of the beige station wagon. "Where'd this come from?"

"It's a loaner from the repair shop. Mine's on the fritz."

"So what's in it I have to see?"

"I'll show you," Vance said. "Com'ere."

As he leaned down to open the door on the driver's side, a padded black body leapt out of the back, pinned Hal's arms behind his back and tied his wrists together with a bungee cord. "Gag him quick!" the voice whispered.

Vance pulled out the scarf he had lifted from Susie's coat closet a week ago when they were all still speaking and tied it harshly in place.

Together Vance and Carla thrust Hal onto the floor of the back seat. "Stay down there," Vance told him. "Stay down out of sight or I swear to God I'll come back there and stand on your face."

It thrilled him to hear his own fury. Was it justice he was after, or something sweeter, something that reached back to their boyhood, to the petty cruelties of adolescence? Sometimes a cigar…is chust a cigar, he said to himself.

By prearrangement, Carla drove. Vance rode in the passenger seat beside her, half turned to keep an eye on his twin in the back.

"We have at least three hours to kill. Don't say anything, just drive. How's the tank?"

Carla gestured at the gauge. She'd thought of that and topped off before picking Vance up at his place. The wagon was a Rent-a-Wreck she'd gotten in Napara. Either of their cars might have been recognized driving around.

They spent the longest three hours of their lives cruising the crowded freeways. There was no radio to soothe them; Vance had a terrible case of the jitters. "For God's sake look out for that nut!" he'd call out. "Let him pass you!" And then, five minutes later, "Be careful! Stay in your lane," he'd cry, even though Carla had swerved not at all.

Daylight waned slowly, grudgingly. Carla had pulled off the ski mask and watch cap before she slipped behind the wheel, and she was careful not to offer her profile to the back of the car. Even with a wig it would be taking a chance. Vance probably had nothing to fear from his twin. The abduction could be passed off as a family vendetta, a prank, whatever. He could blackmail Hal into silence once this was over. But in her case, not only was her residency at the Riva Foundation on the line, she'd be up on a kidnapping and intent-to-do-bodily-harm charge before you could say monkey-do. She was sweating profusely under her stuffed 38-cup bra. Rivulets of sweat were running under the two layers of ski sweaters designed to enlarge her torso.

As darkness fell, they turned and drove back to the lab parking lot. The grad assistant who did the evening feed had come and gone, probably anxious to get that chore over with before heading out to party the night away. Somebody had left an ancient black pickup in the student lot; probably a bunch of kids had convened here and departed as a group to greener pastures. Hal's car was still parked in the Director's space. It looked lonely, standing as if on guard.

Carla pulled in behind the building.

"We'll walk from here," Vance said, shouldering a bulky knapsack. I'm not risking tire tracks."

Between them they forced a moaning Hal to stumble across the chaparral toward the distant pit. By design, there was no path. The location of the pit was a closely guarded secret. Only those participating directly in the experiment knew where it was.

The sky overhead was cloudy. There would be no moon. A distant hum rose from the freeway, steady and reassuring. The order of things still prevailed elsewhere. Vance carried a rope ladder nonchalantly coiled over one shoulder, a fireman with no fire in sight.

At the pit, Vance unfastened the bungee cord and released the gag. He hesitated a moment, feeling something unfamiliar catch in his chest, something rather like pity or revulsion. *Am I my brother's keeper?* Then he recovered himself and forced Hal to precede him down the pliant rope rungs. Three feet from the bottom he ordered him to jump.

"Let go of the rope, you bastard, or I'll break both your hands."

It was no trick to catch the bottom rung up in one hand, then ascend, looping the ladder up as he climbed. At the top he retrieved the knapsack from where he had set it down.

"Here's your sleeping bag and provisions." He threw

down the bedroll and ground cloth, a plastic liter of water and a loaf of day-old Wonder bread.

Hal moaned some response but his words didn't reach the top.

"Welcome to the deprivation experiment on a Higher Ape." Vance slid the plywood cover three-quarters closed and laid the metal grate in place on top of it.

He and Carla didn't speak walking back.

We'll meet at the canyon," Carla said, as Vance unlocked Hal's car with the keys he'd taken from his brother's jacket pocket. He slid in behind the wheel of the '99 BMW.

"Driving this'll be a first," he said.

The gravel margin at the foot of the canyon was a favorite place for making out. It wasn't an official parking lot but ran east-west, a wide beachhead for lovers and climbers. There were no romantic couples as yet. A red Honda was parked discreetly behind a manzanita tree. Vance pulled the BMW in alongside it, leaving just enough space for the owner of the Honda to back out. He tucked the keys on top of the sun visor on the driver's side and joined Carla in the station wagon.

"Home, James," he said.

XII

THERE WAS NO POINT in yelling for help, he knew that much. Friday night there wouldn't be a soul around the lab. The students had all gone home for the Easter recess. The few little bastards who had chosen not to leave town were racing off to frat parties or beer joints with their dates and then back to their dorms or off-campus apartments for a long night of sex. And there was Felicity, alone in the cabin in the canyon, if she got that far. She'd be wondering plenty by now, wondering where the hell he was. He hoped she was frantic with worry.

The thing was, he desperately needed to take a crap. Jesus, he really had to…. Well, he was an old camper, he could deal with this. But no tool to scoop a hole with, no tool but his bare hands. The clay was hard packed, in his urgency he barely managed to dent it with his bare hands and after he'd extruded a smelly dump there was nothing to wipe his ass with. Nothing to cover his manure with, either.

The monkeys, he remembered, always shat in one corner in a pile. The pile expanded like a pyramid over the course of a week if the cages weren't cleaned. A week…. Animals are unable to anticipate. They never knew what was coming next. After the first twenty-four hours of terror and exhaustion from trying to climb the walls, most of them simply gave up and lay curled in fetal position waiting to die. It was weird the way they even stopped accepting food and water, never even looked up after the first two or three days. The thing to look for in the blood was some significant endocrinological change. He knew it was there. If he could just keep up the experiments, he was sure he was on the verge of a real breakthrough.

He put the water bottle and loaf of bread in the opposite corner, working his way by feel in the pitch dark. He couldn't see a goddamn thing any more, it must be clouding over. He patted his way to the sleeping bag, gingerly untied the strings and rolled it out. The space was roughly five by five, big enough to stretch out in, at least on the hypotenuse. As he lay back he felt something soft flatten under his head. Christ! The shit pile.

That goddamn son of a bitch Vance Elias, he'd like to kill him. He *would* kill him, once he got out of here. He'd go to L.A. or San Diego or Las Vegas and buy a gun, he who had never fired so much as a starter pistol, he'd buy a .38 and learn how to load it and cock it and by Christ he would kill the fucker.

It made him feel better, planning to murder his twin. Growing up, he'd hated having to share a room with him. His books, his seashells, his rock collection all neatly labelled. Once in a fit of pique he'd spread the shells out on the floor on Vance's side and stamped them to shards under his football cleats. How he'd loathed Vance's serenity posters warring with his Jeff Beck and Jimi Hendrix. Loathed his little book light so he could read his Dostoevsky all night, despised even the ear plugs he inserted to dampen the throb of Hal's electric guitar. And before that, when they were little kids, Vance always took the rap for their misdeeds. He was the one who got sent away from the table or banished from the tv, except for one occasion when he, Hal, had gotten hauled over their father's knee and spanked with a cooking spoon.

When they were very little, he had to admit he was grateful for a brother to keep the monsters under the bed at bay, to balance his weight on the playground seesaw, a brother to catch and return the softball, bat the shuttlecock, race side by side with him into the waves at Harvey's Point. How he had detested that tacky little crackerbox house in Levittown! How determined he was to break out, be somebody, make his mark. And he was, he had. He was Harold Baranoff, Ph.D., Director of the Edward A. Graysmith Behavioral Sciences Laboratory in Montandino, California, and what was Van Baran? A truncated name, a flash-in-the-pan novelist with two other mediocre books behind him, both out of print, and a year-long, mile-thick writer's block.

Why in God's name he had offered him the Graysmith guest cottage he'd never know. Put it down to his better instincts, but there *were* no better instincts. Envy, revenge, an enhanced sense of superiority, these things Hal understood. But a good deed, a gift to a twin brother down on his luck, that sort of thing belonged in Rick Enslin's aborted altruism study. Cashiering him had been the right thing to do. There was no such thing as altruism. Enlightened self-interest, maybe. Little kids learn early how to put the spin on interpersonal relations. They see adults going at it every day, trading off pity and sympathy for respect and affection. They may not have the vocabulary to express it, but the instinct for doing well by doing good is there from the start.

If you wanted to look at motives, what about Carla, the fiber artist at the Riva Foundation? She and Vance were both involved in that animal rights movement, those do-gooders who were trying to shut him down. Pretty soon the whole town would be coming after him with tar and feathers. Was she really all that pure? Let's liberate the animals and exterminate the fur industry and eat only beans and turnips, sure. Well, the squirrels hadn't got them all, as his father used to say. He had read about an Indian sect, the Jains, who wore gauze masks over their noses and mouths to screen out any insects they might otherwise inadvertently destroy just while they were walking around. The Jains, the article had said, ate only plant matter. They wouldn't even eat any root vegetables for fear of disturbing worms or maggots in the earth around them. Crazy, purely certifiably crazy. It was crazy to be thinking about them, too.

The night dragged on and on. He lay as at the bottom of a well, surprisingly grateful for his sleeping bag even if it was flattened out on his own feces. He had wrapped his shoes up in his trousers to form a blocky sort of pillow. In his jacket, from which Vance had extracted his key ring, he'd found the final third of a roll of Tums. He was thrilled with the discovery. He ate one for dessert after the bread and saved the others for later. For the indeterminate later, which he could indeed anticipate.

No one except Felicity would miss him for at least three more days. Susie wasn't due back until Tuesday, so the kids wouldn't return to the house until then, either. They had been expressly forbidden to go in there without one parent or the other in residence. And Felicity would never find him. She'd never think to look for him out here, she hardly knew anything about this ongoing experiment. Just that he had a big government grant. Just that he drove a new BMW, wore Calvin Klein boxers and favored Sulka ties. He felt a pang of regret for the wild weekend he'd planned in the canyon, the trouble he'd taken to assemble supplies, give her directions, a key to the cabin. Schlepping those gourmet foods up there he had felt young again, lighthearted, full of new energy.

Really, what else did she know about him, she who sat in the front row of his Contemporary Models in Cognitive Behavior, she who was his tutee and soon to be his teaching assistant? Just that he was an imaginative lover, that he made having sex into wonderful performance art, that he allowed, encouraged her to play out her favorite role. She was the dominatrix, leaving ridges on his ass with her butter paddle, diving into his hole with her enema tip, drenching his cock with green soap solution, then none too gently scouring him clean as he lay handcuffed to the bedstead. His own Big Nurse. He had taught her how to prolong each of their orgasms with amytal ampules lined up within easy reach under the pillow, and lately he was teaching her how to use the scarf as a noose around his neck to be tightened just to the verge of unconsciousness, so that when he came it was with prolonged and explosive force.

Susie had never enjoyed games in bed. Her inner landscape was an arctic wasteland. She skimmed along it oblivious to crevasses, blind to danger. She wasn't inhibited, although he had accused her of that; it was just that she was wholly without artifice. Her creative juices were scant. Because she couldn't paint or compose music, sculpt or write, she had taken up weaving. Weaving, for chrissake! What did that require? Patience and finger dexterity, as far as he could see. You sat at the loom hour after hour making little movements with your hands and feet going back and forth, back and forth and eventually you had something to hang on the wall or spread out on the floor, and then you didn't want to walk on it.

He had to admit Susie was a totally good person, she was an extraordinary mother of their extraordinary kids. She treated them not just with affection, she listened when they talked, she advised without meddling. She protected Lottie as long as she could, for the kids' sake and for her own; hadn't they all made Lottie a member of the family? They'd even put up with Drew, who was prickly and deferential by turns.

He loved Susie. As marriages go, theirs was companionable, functional, he with his career, she allotting her energy to parenting, chaperoning, serving at hospice, and so on. The columns she wrote for the *Gourmet Gazette* were something she seemed able to do with the left hand. She rarely tried out new spices at home; he didn't care much for curries and cilantro. Although right now he'd give anything for her couscous with unidentifiable objects on top of it.

Whereas what he felt for Felicity was lust. Lust everlasting? He felt a hard-on coming and it made him whimper. Lying here on top of his own ordure, smelling it, lying here at the bottom of a five-by-five hole in the ground with an erection. Yes, he *would* kill Vance, conspire to kill him, rub him out, finish him off. He would.

Toward morning it started to rain. It rarely rained this late in the year on the chaparral, but occasionally when the Pineapple Express brought moisture in from the ocean, an appreciable rain would scour the valley and move up into the canyons, often bringing cloudbursts to the mountains. It would have been snug at the cabin with a crackling fire of pinyon burning, a bottle of burgundy at hand, a lazy long undisciplined day to amuse each other. Perhaps he would play with Felicity's remarkable red hair, sectioning it and braiding it the way she wore it as a little girl.

He was cold and wet and deeply depressed. He clung to his murderous rage like a drowning man, and it warmed him somewhat.

An intermittent drizzle fell much of the day. He relieved himself in the same corner, then crouched in the opposite one where the plywood overhead afforded some shelter, although drips streamed down the metal walls and puddled under him. In spite of his misery he was hungry, and he partook again of the tasteless bread, drank from the bottle, and topped off his meal with his next-to-last Tums. He sucked it slowly, making it last as long as he could.

That was another thing about Vance. He could make an

ice cream cone last forever. Hal's would have been licked and crunched and completed and there was Vance still fastidiously licking and turning and tamping the sweetness down into the sugar cone. Even offering him another lick, a nibble. Once, he'd snatched the cone away and shoved the remnants in his own mouth. Unluckily, their father caught him in the act. When they got home from the Boardwalk, he was spanked with the spoon. He hadn't thought of that in what? Forty years, forty-five? The memory bank. The retrieval system: the five senses. In this instance, taste, hunger.

He heard Vance arrive in the early dark, heard his footsteps squishing one by one, then saw the beam of the flashlight play along the wall of his hole, angle down onto the earth, play over his sleeping bag, and find his face. He put a hand over his eyes to keep from being blinded.

"Nice and dry down there?"

"Whaddayou think, you motherfucker?"

"Had enough?"

He had the spirit to toss back, "Enough what?"

Vance took a different tack. "I'm dropping you down a package wrapped in your poncho. There's a pen and a pad of paper in it and if you write out a statement disavowing your animal experiments, turning the grant money back to the feds, I'll get you out."

"How the fuck am I supposed to write in the dark?"

"You're not. You're supposed to think about it tonight, compose it the way you did your grant applications. You write it tomorrow morning as soon as you can see. If I like what it says, I'll haul you out tomorrow night."

"You lousy cocksucking shit, you're going to leave me in here another whole day and night? It's soaking wet down here, there's no way I can...," He broke off. "For God's sake, Vance, I'm your *brother*. Get me out of here, if you have a shred of decency left."

It was the wrong tack, he knew it even as he spoke.

"A young monkey drowned in this pit last month. You're a higher ape. Deal with it."

The flashlight clicked off. In the dark, a bundle plopped on his head. He could hear Vance's footsteps receding.

XIII

THEY HAD FOUGHT over what to name the baby. Susie was delirious over her arrival, so besotted with motherhood she insisted on calling her Angela, her one true angel. Hal hated the name. It was overweening, pretentious, it sounded Hispanic, it was Christian. He favored Judith, Deborah, Rebecca. Of course he gave in, how could he hold out against Susie, who had suffered through childbirth, had been literally torn apart by the baby's crowning head.

True, he'd come to resent the overwhelming presence of a baby in their lives. It determined when they ate, slept, went outdoors, had sex — a rare event that caused Susie so much pain that he stopped petitioning her.

Back then in New York they had had a really great sublet, a floor-through on West 117th. Vance came to visit, he'd been out on book tour, he looked shaggy and pleased with himself, with leather patches on his sports coat and a rough shock of hair that ran down into his beard. Vance wore only jeans, preferably out at one knee, a blue workshirt à la français open at the neck, and a thick belt from which a Swiss Army knife dangled. His workboots were mustard brown, stained as if he had gone to battle in them. He looked as casually disreputable as a Hollywood thug.

Having Vance there seemed to cheer Susie up, it was just a few weeks after the baby died. She was crazy with grief, there was no other word for it. She seemed to think he'd had something to do with it, he'd smothered her out of jealousy or rage when she wouldn't stop crying. What he'd done that day when she cried endlessly was simply to go down the hall to the living room, put on a Mozart quartet to drown out her little catlike wails, and get started on a stack of undergrad papers he was grading for Psych I. At some point he must have dozed off; when he woke, the apartment was quiet.

He got Susie professional help for postpartum depression, that's what it was. She went from day to day as if packed in bubble wrap; there was no reaching her. When he and the shrink discussed alternative methods of treatment she seemed to come to. Almost a whole year had gone by.

□

They were fraternal twins, he and Vance. He was stockier, with broader shoulders and feet a full shoe-size bigger than his brother. He toed out as he walked, Vance used to say that he looked like an army drill master. Vance's face was narrower: wide-set eyes that always looked a bit startled, or at the least, wary; aquiline nose with flared nostrils, square chin. His lips were rosy as a girl's, and when he spoke, a dimple appeared at the righthand corner of his mouth. Partly to obscure the dimple Vance had grown a beard. It straggled in at first, but by the time he was in his twenties it had thickened to a luxuriant bush. Now, at fifty-one, curly gray clusters had invaded the brown nest.

Growing up, they were not the only twins in Levittown. The Becker boys were formidable tennis players. The Adcocks both scored in the high 700's on their math SATs. Some of the boy twins flaunted their relationship, others bore it with resignation. For the most part, they chose different shirts, disparate jackets.

The girl twins were more likely to dress the same. Beth and Becca Burlingame clung to each other as if to inform the world that they needed no other friends even though Hal suspected they longed for them. Back then, girl twins were more stigmatized by their twinship. People were always peering at them in mock dismay, asking, "Which one are *you*?" even if the differences between them were perfectly obvious. Hal and Vance sped off in different directions, shucking kinship along with their undershirts as they raced to join their separate friends. Brotherhood was a curse to each of them.

They were the earliest crop of baby boomers, born just after World War II drew to a close, mostly to returning servicemen and their wives. Levittown was square boxes of houses with twigs for trees, a new community laid out by an enterprising developer on what had then been cheap Long Island acreage. Safe and sunny, competitive in lawns and pocket-size flower gardens, it soon grew large enough to acquire its own schools, pharmacies and supermarket.

He and Vance shared a bedroom with bunk beds, switching off top and bottom on the first of every month. Hal, older by twelve minutes, dominated Vance. He favored black light, rock and roll posters. His unmade bed sagged beneath the weight of his electric guitar, amplifiers, and leather jacket. Vance put up framed landscapes, calm vistas of palm trees and oceans, red barns and snowy pastures.

When they were eight and he was into matches, Hal remembered that he set fire to the Harrisons' backyard. It was some time in the fall; the grass was very dry and flamed up magnificently. Why was it he never got caught? In fact, he turned in the alarm himself and stood there lying to the cops.

❑

Because graduation day was sunny and hot, he arrived naked under the rented gown. He went around to selected guests and asked, "How'd you like to shake hands with a bare-assed graduate of Levittown High?" And he'd pulled his robe up a little to show off his hairy shins and wiggled his backside so the robe eddied around him.

Vance walked off with the Latin Prize, the Honor Society Medal and the Goldstone Prize for Excellence in Literature. They marched in lockstep back out of the auditorium, not speaking till they reached the dressing room.

"What a stupid exhibitionist jerk you are," he remembered Vance saying.

"Fuck you, little brother."

Nothing much had changed.

XIV

REUBEN AND RACHEL were inseparable from the start. They were a healthy antidote to Hal's own bitter memories. He was baffled by their spontaneous affection for one another and perplexed by their altruism, a concept he had always regarded as suspect.

In the babies' first year, the Baranoffs moved to Montandino, and the twins made an effortless adjustment to southern Californian mores. Their hair bleached out to dirty blond, their pale skin tanned. They graduated to eating mashed up avocadoes and lime sorbet.

For a long time Susie wouldn't hear of leaving the twins in anyone else's care. After the baby's mysterious crib death, nothing would persuade her to allow a stranger to look after these astonishing infants. And then Lottie, wonderful, slovenly, loving Lottie came into their lives, sent by the Chief of Police, of all people.

Some people called Digger Martinez the Eagle of Montandino; there was nothing he and Theresa weren't aware of. Sometimes it was a subliminal awareness, a prickle at the base of his neck that warned Digger of events to come. Sometimes there was no warning. But when the rescue squad was called out in the middle of the night because the Graysmith Director's wife was seized with terrible stomach pains, he was only minutes behind. An emergency appendectomy was performed three hours later, leaving an overwhelmed Dr. Baranoff with toddlers to care for.

Digger knew a middle-aged motherly woman who was living with her son nearby. It was taking a chance, but she'd been on the wagon for almost six months now. There weren't a lot of other options; he guessed he could put her in touch with the Director. And so Lottie came into the Baranoffs' lives. Who could have predicted Lottie's fate? Who could have guessed the shadow cast by her eccentric grown son Drew, who came and went like a ghost in their lives, first reproaching, then blaming Hal for her addiction?

They were a strange pair, Lottie and Drew. Joined at the hip, Hal liked to say, shaking his head. He marveled that two generations could sustain such a tight connection. Although he honored his father and mother like a good Jewish son, although he phoned them back East every Sunday and flew them to California to visit twice a year, there was a healthy emotional and chronological distance between him and his parents. Not this unhealthy in-flux relationship Lottie and Drew had. Sometimes Drew was the parent, sometimes the child. And sometimes, coming upon them, you would almost mistake them for lovers.

Susie and Lottie became co-conspirators, doting on the twins, revelling in their sunny dispositions. They conferred over suitable toys, appropriate books, the approach to toilet training. The household ran smoothly, Lottie discreetly behind the scenes when Susie and Hal were together, but ready to take charge whenever they went out.

Twinship acquired a new luster for Hal. He began to think that he and Vance had become combatants, like rats, from overcrowding in that little box of a house, and in the zoo of Levittown. Their small bedroom had been a cage, their parents poorly trained, if not indifferent, keepers. He and Susie were attentive, admirable parents; their children would turn out differently.

⌐

The book tour fizzled. Vance's third novel was

remaindered in less than a year. He hired out as a tutor to
the rich sons of wealthy Moroccan merchants, despising
himself for abandoning his own work.

For several years he wandered from Algeria to Egypt,
from France to England. When he was offered an appoint-
ment as writer-in-residence at Thoreau, a small liberal arts
college in New Hampshire, he jumped at it. He thought it
would help to get back to the natural world. The appoint-
ment came with a fully furnished log cabin and a woodshed
neatly piled with split hardwood. Once he had hung up feed-
ers and a suet cake he became the custodian of more than a
dozen species of birds.

The students at Thoreau were earnest, depressed, and
only minimally ambitious. When they weren't altering their
moods with marijuana or coke or prescription drugs, they
praticed a weary cynicism. To Vance they seemed younger
than he could imagine himself ever having been. More subject to mood swings, alienated beyond his farthest
imaginings. He felt helpless to guide them out of their mi-
asma.

For distraction, he hiked through the surrounding wood-
lands, climbed granite ledges; one day he had discovered a
tree stand well situated for viewing through his zoom lens.

Someone was climbing toward him, a small, no longer
young woman, slightly built, a little out of breath from the
incline. Her face wore a snub nose and smile crinkles at the
corners of a generous mouth.

She had reached the foot of the tree and called up to
him. "What are you doing up there?"

"What am I doing up here?" He held out his Minolta.
"What does it look like? Who are you?"

"I live down there." She gestured behind her. "Don't you
know it's hunting season? Being out here without a gun is
dangerous."

"So what about you? Why are you out here without a rifle?"

"Oh, I'm trying to find some hunters."

"Hunters? What for?"

"To interfere with their stalking."

"Interfere? You mean get in the way of their shooting?"

"That's it."

"And then what happens?"

"Then I ask them why they want to kill deer."

"What do they say?"

"Usually they cuss me out, call me a bleeding heart, tell me the deer would starve if guys like them didn't hunt them every fall."

"And what do you say to that?"

"Well, I try to educate them. I tell them that's just a line of propaganda the gun lobby puts out, that if the deer weren't hunted to death they wouldn't reproduce so heavily."

He was incredulous. "Aren't you afraid you'll get shot?"

"That's the point. We need the publicity."

"And you're willing to get shot for that?"

"Shot *at*, anyway. Mind if I come up?"

He held a hand out to her.

"Carla Strombaugh," she said, sitting alongside him.

"Carla Strombaugh. I know I've seen that name somewhere. My name's Vance Baranoff."

She nodded an acknowledgement. "So what's with the camera?"

"I'm strictly an amateur. Actually, I'm a writer. When I'm writing. What about you?"

"I'm a weaver. I do wall hangings, runners, things like that."

"You're the fiber artist in the Chester cottage? I saw some of your stuff on exhibit at the town hall."

"Guilty."

"Well, we're neighbors. I live just about a mile from you in the Thoreau College cabin."

"Oh, so you're the writer-in-residence this year?"

He grimaced. "Let's just say I'm in residence. Whether I'm writing or not is a moot point."

She sympathized. "It's lousy when you run dry, I know."

"You mean fiber artists have...what'll we call it, wool block?"

She flashed him an appreciative smile. "You bet."

"So when you're blocked you wander around the woods on the first day of the season."

"Not exactly. From time to time animal rights takes precedence over art."

He and Carla got together frequently after their first encounter.

"Nothing personal," she said. "But I'm not interested in a romantic relationship."

"You have nothing to worry about," he assured her. "My libido is at an all-time low."

Usually it was Vance who hiked across the intervening ridge; sometimes, though, she came knocking with a bottle of wine.

They commiserated with each other. She said that she had more projects pending than she could manage. "This gallery in Soho is hounding me. It's gotten so I see knots in the warp in my sleep."

He confessed that he was at an impasse. "I'm $15,000 in hock to my publisher for an advance and I think the well is dry."

"How do you know?"

"I tore up an entire chapter this morning. It's so fucking awful. I hate the guy I'm writing about."

"Who is he?"

"Me."

"Want some advice?"

"Sure."

"Stay outside a lot." She gave him an open-faced smile.

Bit by bit, some of the facts about her animal rights activities leaked out. She told him pridefully that she had been arrested five times. "Also, I've gone to jail."

Vance was intrigued. "Arrested for what?"

"Criminal trespass. Theft. Destruction of government property. Disorderly conduct. Resisting an officer." She ticked them off on her fingers.

"Come on, Carla, don't bullshit me. Theft of what?"

"Cats, for one. We broke into a lab at Preston University and stole six cats they'd been injecting with various paralyzing agents, cats that were going to be 'harvested'— that's the euphemism they use for killing them."

"That's right. I remember reading something about it in the paper, two, three years ago?"

"Five years, actually. Right."

"What else'd you steal?"

"Mink. Primates. Dogs, most of them family pets that were picked up on the streets and sold to biomedical labs."

"So what was the jail sentence for?"

"Oh, that was in Michigan, long ago, the night we broke into the university."

"You broke in?"

"You always try to commit your sabotage at night. We destroyed their files on mink research, they claimed it was thirty years' worth."

"You just ripped up the papers?"

She laughed. "No, better than that. We set them on fire. But three of us got caught and the cops were really brutal."

"What'd they do to you?"

"Two of them beat me up in the back of the squad car.

Bruised one kidney, ruptured my spleen."

"Did you sue?"

"Are you kidding? In a hostile environment like that?"

"Are you still… protesting?"

"I'm a brick-throwing survivor of the animal liberation movement. But I don't do actions any more. With my record, I feel I can't risk spending years and years behind bars."

"But you still care."

"I still care. But I don't want to bore you."

"Jesus," Vance said. "Here I'm farting around trying to write a novel and you've already lived two or three."

"'To thine own self be true,' you know?"

"I admire commitment," Vance said. "It's what I'm short on."

❒

In July he flew out to see his brother, that stranger, in California. Enough time had passed so that they were cast as new acquaintances, politely interested, while not involved in, each other's lives. Their father had died several years ago. Their mother had resettled in a condo in Sarasota. They'd shared these disjunctions and relocations equably, dividing the residual furniture, the few china treasures.

The old twinship bond had dissolved, taking with it the ancient and savage animosity of their adolescent years. In its place, Vance felt, a tentative relationship was budding. They could quite simply be brothers.

Hal casually held out the possibility of Vance's relocating temporarily. Perhaps the desert would stimulate, harass him to new efforts. Hal felt he could afford to be magnanimous in his southern California kingdom. One twin succeeds; the other fails. From the top of the ladder he dangled the olive branch.

After one more season of coming up blank time after time against the pale green screen of his computer, Vance packed his bags.

Hal offered him the Graysmith Lab guest house, a salmon pink adobe cottage just out of the valley, a thousand feet up into the great dry hills. There were no neighbors to peer in. In fact, except for one other adobe structure, a large compound belonging to the Ravi Foundation a bit to the north and east, Vance could see nothing but sere landscape dotted with scrub oak and alder.

Graysmith, along with Maartens Theological School and the Hammerling Engineering Institute, formed a triangle of higher learning on the hardscrabble chaparral. The town of Montandino fed well on this unlikely triumvirate. Service jobs bloomed for the sons and daughters of the local Chicanos who cooked and cleaned, repaired cars for, and laid tile in the homes of the tenured academics.

Montandino itself was little more than six square blocks of boutiques and bookstores, a drugstore, and half a dozen eateries. A lone church, nondenominational, sent up its pencilled spire. Picket fences, brick sidewalks, and two blocks illuminated by gas lights all contributed to the faux New England air of the town.

The locals went to Napara to market and buy supplies. Napara, twenty miles away, had a weekly newspaper, a hardware store, two bars, a liquor store, and a steady if turgid economy as the gateway to the resorts of the desert, thirty miles farther east.

The Ravi Foundation, a combination artists' retreat and community outreach group, was the gift of a Hungarian duo piano team, now both deceased. In the fifties they had retired to Montandino, Josef with asthma and Poulina with arthritis. They were generous eccentrics, supporting every artistic endeavor from papier-maché masks to musical scholarships.

Carla's studio took up almost half the building. The huge, airy room with thick stucco walls and big glass doors on the north side reminded her of the lofts of New York, especially the cavernous ones in Brooklyn where three or four painters or sculptors shared spaces that had once held massive textile machinery. Her bedroom, bath and kitchen, all in a line like a shotgun apartment, winged out on the east side.

About six weeks after she'd settled in, she was driving to the Food Co-op when someone walking a Dalmatian in the rain caught her eye. He was coming up the clay road that wound past the Foundation and there was something familiar about the way the man moved, something tightly wound, yet limber.

"There really *are* only five thousand people in the world and they keep meeting each other over and over," Vance said, when she pulled alongside him.

She opened the window on his side. "My God! What are you doing here?"

He grinned. "We have to stop meeting like this."

"Isn't this crazy? But what are you doing out here?"

"Same thing you are, I guess."

"Working on the book? How's it going?"

"Better since I took me out of it. What about you?"

"Weaving big wall pieces." She gestured toward the Foundation building behind her. "That's an artists' colony. I have a studio in it and a huge floor loom. Free."

"Far out," he said.

"I have to say, Vance, I love seeing you with a dog."

"Why, what did you think I was, an animal hater?"

She turned off the ignition, got out, and stooped down to pat the Dalmatian. "How old is he? What's his name?"

"Arthur. Nobody knows, exactly. About a year. The Chief

of Police gave him to me."

"Digger Martinez? The Eagle of Montandino? He just about runs this town."

"Yeah, well, he picked him up on the highway a couple of weeks ago, very dehydrated and skinny. No collar, no tags. Actually, that guy who cruises around town in his pickup, Drew something-or-other, found him and took him to the Chief."

"Imagine giving a dog like this up."

"The hypothesis is he was a lab dog that got away. They use a lot of Dals, you know, because they're such high producers of uric acid."

"There's no lab within a hundred miles that uses dogs," she said definitively.

"You've seen to that, I guess?"

"No, but I know which labs do what. There's a professor here who's starting in on primates, did you know that?"

"You mean at Graysmith? I thought that was a nursery school."

"It is. But the director's branching out, going from early childhood development to maternal-infant bonding in macaques."

"Macaques? That's a bird."

"You're thinking of macaws. These are rhesus macaques, an Indian monkey. They're what Jonas Salk used."

"You mean the polio vaccine?"

Carla nodded. "You know, it's uncanny. You remind me so much of this guy."

"I'm his twin. That's how I got out here. I'm living in the lab's visitors' quarters."

"You're Hal Baranoff's twin? But you're nothing alike."

Vance laughed. "You just got through saying how much I resemble him."

"Not exactly a resemblance." Carla thought a minute.

"The same features but they're assembled a little...more loosely. I mean, I wouldn't have any more trouble telling you apart than your dog does."

Vance grinned. "You don't have his nose."

"Do you know anything about your brother's project?"

"Not really. Hal's big on behavior, though. He's probably expiating all the bad things he did as a teenager."

"Acting out, maybe. Not expiation."

"So what's he doing, actually?"

"Redoing the same old isolation experiments Harlow did thirty, forty years ago, taking infants away from their mothers."

"What the hell for?"

"Well, he can't very well take human infants away, can he? It's against the law. But I suggest you ask him. He says he's studying stress."

XV

HAL HAD WANTED his experiments on rhesus macaques to begin in secret, but monkeys are impossible to hide. His had come from a licensed importer in Florida. They arrived neatly crated, already tested in quarantine for the variety of diseases they could carry. The federal grant money paid to establish an entire floor of steel cages, zinc-lined bins for their food, and ample dollars for graduate assistants to participate in the experiments, draw blood, keep notes, and computerize the results.

The idea was not original with him, but it had grown logically out of his early work with small children. Separation anxiety was not well understood. What Hal was trying to do was to unravel the body chemistry of stress induced by isolation so that this new information could be applied to human conditions. The chemistry of alarm flooded the monkey bloodstreams with a hormone known as cortisol. By comparing the cortisol levels in varying situations — in cases where the babies were totally isolated from their mothers, in cases where they could see but not touch their mothers behind a plastic shield, in cases where their mothers were absent but other companions were still present — Hal hoped to obtain evidence that could be extrapolated to humans. Everyone knew there was a powerful connection between human emotions and physical wellbeing, but how to factor this information into a study of the immune system was the question.

Rachel was the most vulnerable.

"Don't go giving them names. They're not pets and they're not to be treated as pets," he lectured.

"But they're so...helpless! It just looks so cruel, Daddy. I don't see how you can do it, day after day."

"Don't make me out to be The Butcher of Belsen, Ray. These are valid, vital scientific experiments, the results are going to save human lives someday. Lift people out of their depressions and hallucinations, help them back into society."

"So if you take baby monkeys from their mothers, drop them down into your steel chamber somewhere out behind the lab and leave them there until they're drawn up into desperate little balls of fur, that's going to save lives?"

"Yes, ultimately. What I learn from these experiments will show a pattern that can be applied to human self-abusers, people who pick their skin open, bang their heads on walls, eat glass, and so on."

"I don't believe that at all."

"You're just not mature enough to grasp the concept," he said, knowing how much she would resent the remark. "This is a very new scientific field...."

"The science of sadism? I thought it was centuries-old."

He had to admire her spunk.

"Psychoneuroimmunology," he finished, but she had already walked out of the room.

The trouble was, research on primates had gotten a bad name. First, there was Zennarelli's fiasco in Silver Springs studying head injuries inflicted on baboons, the disastrous videotape that got out, showing lab assistants mocking the brain-damaged ones, dangling them by their crippled arms, making up speeches in which they pleaded to be rescued.

Then there was Harlow with his crucifixion chair, simply a restraining device for immobilizing the subject, but it had aroused such an outcry that the experiment was abandoned. And as if that weren't enough, he had to go and name his method of immobilizing the females in estrus to test the sexual responses of abnormal male monkeys that came out of isolation experiments. He seemed to delight in publicizing it as a rape rack. Maybe Rachel was right— the guy certainly came off as a sadist. Just grist for the mill of the animal advocacy groups.

Hal's own submerged chamber — Harlow had called his "the pit of despair"— was of necessity located a good quarter of a mile from Graysmith itself. For one thing, Graysmith had never been intended to house lab animals. The third floor had been modified for this purpose; even so, the soundproofing was inadequate. The ground floor was entirely taken up with playschool and kindergarten facilities. The second floor housed administrative offices, classrooms, computers and library facilities. The isolated infant monkeys cried so piteously and loudly that the pit had to be strategically located at a safe distance. It was dug by a single backhoe operating at night, shored up with steel plates that slanted inward. The top was partially covered with plywood to keep out the rain, and the whole was enclosed in steel grating. No one was supposed to know where the pit was, but it didn't take a brain surgeon to figure it out.

To the few staffers who protested the experiments, Baranoff insisted, "What these will tell us about human depression, its duration, its reversal, is absolutely groundbreaking information on the treatment of mental disorder. Behavioral research contributes significantly to the improvement of human health." But he wasn't entirely sure he believed it himself.

XVI

Easter Sunday morning Montandino's Chief of Police belted out *gloria in excelsis Deo* in the shower while Theresa started the coffee. They both liked it thick and in copious quantities. They had talked about going to midnight Mass the night before, but Digger admitted it was too hard to stay up that late, and Theresa, who had secretly rented a video and was planning chicken fajitas, was quick to concur. She had put on her big flowered housecoat, the one their daughter Aurelia had brought her from Hawaii. She popped a bowl of fiesta popcorn, and after supper they settled contentedly in front of the blue light to watch an old John Wayne film.

Getting up early came easily to them both. Whenever he had the option, Digger always selected the early watch on board ship year after year. And organizing for the Farm Workers Union all those years meant keeping workers' hours; Theresa was well acquainted with sunrise.

The church they belonged to, Holy Name, was only half an hour away in Napara, unless you were trying to get there at rush hour. Early Mass on Easter was at 7. Incredibly, Montandino was too Anglo in attitude to support a Catholic Church of its own, even though most of the town was Chicano. Diego Martinez preferred the word Latino. He was, after all, third generation. But he shied away from calling himself Spanish-American. That term had a snobbish edge to it, the thin blade of an ultra-respectability he had no wish to lay claim to.

Montandino's United Church, all-purpose nonsectarian, was holding one Easter service, at 11 a.m. A few years ago there had been a move to promote a midnight service there as well, an hour better suited to the social needs of the parishioners, but the effort petered out. In a small town, heavy drinking and adulterous acts coalesce around Saturday nights. And what was Easter to most of them anyway, Digger mused. Eggs and rabbits and fancy chocolates. Though he himself had taken the United Church minister and his wife to midnight Mass at Holy Name last year.

It made Digger a little self-conscious, the way they were so heavily ecumenical. Well, he supposed it was the way he was raised, defensive about his religion, the way Jews are in a mostly Christian community. It was a good thing, this kind of overlap, what the minister called religious fellowship. The way Passover and Easter connected, for instance. Digger was a grown man before he found out that the Last Supper depicted Christ at a Seder. Now he too had eaten the cold fish, the chopped apples and nuts, he'd raised his glass of sweet wine four times the way Christ did. Too bad Dr. B. was so... confrontational. Couldn't hold four glasses of wine without getting aggressive. It was hard to believe that he and Vance came out of the same womb. But it was a good thing to partake of other ways to worship. Easter filled Digger with high moral fervor.

Coming back from Mass, Digger cruised down the main street, a habit he clung to. Digger claimed he could sniff out the day's temper, as it were, this way. Thirty years in this town had made the village a pack of Tarot cards for him to read. An influx of fancy sports cars from the coast spelled trouble. Bikers blatting down the bare streets, temptation. Fog, smog, drizzle or downpour indicated he would have no appreciable business to conduct. Southern Californians were very sensitive to the nuances of the weather. They stayed indoors the minute things got nasty.

It was 8:30; too early for the United Church service. The

bakery was closed. A stack of Sunday papers sat outside the pharmacy, which would open at 10, the sign said. Out of the corner of his eye Digger saw a little red Honda streak past at the top of Main Street, along Foothill Avenue, gateway to the hills, followed by Drew Deveraux's familiar battered black pickup. He shook his head. This was probably the last Easter Deveraux would see. Meanwhile, prosperous Montandino still had its sidewalks pulled up tight. Digger had taken on this job when he retired from the Navy, relieved at last of the constant nausea the sea induced in him.

Montandino was a quiet community then. The Hammerling School was in its infancy. The Behavioral Lab had just gotten a modest endowment from the Graysmith fortunes, enough to underwrite the first child development study, and only the fustily conservative Theological School had been a functioning institution for half a century.

They were all Johnny-Come-Latelys, the engineers and psychologists, the restaurateurs, the owners of chic boutiques and the pharmacy, the dry cleaners, the little crammed-to-the-ceiling hardware store, compared to Digger. They had all come to Montandino seeking good health or the solace of a small town untouched by violent crime. The lab, the Institute, the stucco and brick-fronted capacious houses on all the side streets fell under his gaze. His fatherly gaze. He did not see himself as a tyrant or holy fool, though he knew there were some who did. He was a good and concerned citizen in the service of a golden little town. What he felt for Montandino was love. Love, not too strong a word.

Theresa, who had grown up following the crops with her migrant farm worker parents, sometimes chastised him for his complacency.

"You think you belong here," she said. "But just because your grandaddy owned a grocery in Tucson, when push comes to shove, believe me, we're the ones who'll get shoved."

Digger protested. "I've never heard a racist remark in this town. Except for Deveraux, and he spits out mouthfuls automatically, it's like a reflex with him. Kikes, wogs, spics, niggers. He even calls himself a cajun cripple."

"Just because they don't say them to your face doesn't mean they aren't thinking them."

"But they couldn't run this town without me."

Theresa snorted.

Most of Digger's work consisted of directing traffic at high school graduations or driving the cruiser at the head of funeral processions. From time to time he picked up a teenage runaway trying to thumb a ride on the freeway. There were a dozen break-ins a year, almost always local kids. Not too much in the way of drugs that he knew of. He turned a blind eye to marijuana grown in backyards, there was only so much you could do.

And once, ten years ago, on a Sunday as quiet as this one, there had been a murder. A wealthy art dealer's wife had been having an affair with the chef of a chic new restaurant. The wronged husband strangled her in her bed, then stuffed the body in the jacuzzi and left for Mexico. Digger had had to call in the state medical examiner before he dared remove the corpse. He'd seen enough dead bodies in the war, God knows, though he was only a kid then. That was different. That was survival, pure and simple. What he knew about human nature in peacetime was that sometimes passion can flower into hate.

Woolgathering this way, he drove right past their turnoff.

Theresa scolded him. "You're worse than those absent-minded professors!" He had to make a you-ee then and there, and you-ees were illegal even if you were Diego Digger Martinez, Chief of Police.

XVII

VANCE WAITED until it was fully dark Easter Sunday evening. He drove cautiously around the back side of Graysmith, parked on the opposite side of the street down about fifty yards, and eased the rope ladder out of the back seat. Because he felt exposed carrying the ladder around loose, he'd found a Venetian shade box in which it fit exactly. Even so, he really had the jitters. How do you explain walking around with a rope ladder borrowed from a child's tree house? How do you account for slouching furtively across the chaparral this way, trudging in the general direction of nowhere?

He made his way cautiously toward the pit, keeping the flashlight low to the ground, taking care not to create a marked path as he skirted a patch of scrub oak here, a clump of yucca there. Mule deer had grazed the brushy landscape; little clusters of their droppings dotted the soil. He was feeling rotten today, feeling sorry for himself, for his involvement in the kidnap plot even though he still believed in the necessity for hatching it, regretting last Wednesday's altercation with his one and only brother. He should have kept his temper, he was supposed to be the moderate sibling.

It was odd; he didn't feel very guilty about Susie. He had consoled her well after the baby died. What did he do then? He was a coward. He fled. And the second time, after he came back from Europe? The second coming, he thought of it. Well, he didn't think he would run away again.

Some sixth sense had prepared him for what he found at the pit mouth. He felt only a dull sort of shock to discover that the grating and plywood had been laid aside. A crude fabric rope with knots in it was still tied to the base of an adjacent scrub oak. It was amazing that the little tree had held a human weight. He turned his flashlight on and shone it down, down around all four metal sides of the hole. Clearly, Hal was not there. What reflected back were the two empty plastic water bottles, a bread wrapper, and the notebook he'd dropped down with the poncho.

God! Somebody had gotten the bastard out. But who? Who else knew? Not Susie. Maybe Digger. But how would Digger know? Manuel? No way Manuel could, would, morally or immorally. Some passerby out walking his dog? But who in this law-abiding community would brave the No Trespassing signs posted all along the Graysmith margins, especially with the invitingly groomed trails that crisscrossed acres of open town land just across the way?

Still, it could have happened that a stranger passed by. And if it did, he, Vance Baranoff, was in deep trouble by now. He'd better get down there and retrieve the notebook. Get all that other crap out, too, 'specially the poncho or what was left of it, and the sleeping bag. Eventually somebody official was going to look in and wonder, construct a scenario.

He wasn't as good at this as Hal, who, given a rope, could walk up the side of the Empire State building. He had to set up the ladder, climb down, gather up the trash and equipment into one clumsy bundle, climb back one-handed, dismantle the sleeping bag liner/poncho lifeline, and assemble it all into one manageable armload. Lastly he rolled up the ladder and replaced it in its box, which he carried in the crook of his other arm. None of this would have been easy to do by daylight. Picking out the knots one by one in the dark was awkward and frustrating. He stumbled around with his flashlight, taking care not to describe an arc that would be visible from a distance. The walk back out to the road was perilous with his arms full of equipment; without the flashlight he couldn't see to pick out the best route, but he couldn't manage the light along with his other burdens. He was too preoccupied with completing the journey to consider the ramifications of Hal's disappearance. Eventually, though, he came out to the road, and soon after that was in his car heading back to the cottage.

He drove cautiously away from the site without turning his headlights on until he had cleared the bend. Now his heart was hammering in his chest. What had begun as a small act of reprisal had become a possibly public event.

Now he had a missing brother. Any minute now Hal would reappear with Digger and swear out a warrant for his arrest. For kidnapping, for bodily harm, for God knows what other illegal act. He'd try to convince Digger it was a prank. He'd try to keep Carla out of it.

Not till he was back at the cottage did he think to look in the notebook.

There it was, in Hal's inimitable lefthand script. The letters still slanted the wrong way, despite Miss Feinstein's weekly coaching sessions, the a's and b's and d's still wrongly made from bottom to top instead of in the approved style.

"I renounce and recant my research on rhesus macaque and squirrel monkeys and agree to send the animals presently in my laboratory to appropriate animal advocacy groups. I further agree to return the remaining funding to the grant agency or agencies from which it came and not to seek funds in the future for this or other behavioral research involving primates."

He decided to walk over to the Riva Foundation with Arthur; it was important now to keep everything looking casual and ordinary. By now his phone might be tapped. By now the FBI might be on his case. Man walks dog to neighbor's house.

He could see Carla through the kitchen window; he

rapped lightly on the frame and she hurried to let him in.

"How did it go? Did you get him out okay? Did he come through for us?"

"He's not there."

"Not in the pit?"

"Gone. Made some sort of climbing rope out of strips of poncho and the nylon ground cloth of the sleeping bag."

"But someone had to help him! Someone had to be there, tie it to something at the top."

"A very convenient tree."

"Who do you think?"

"I don't have a clue. Could have been just somebody who came along, you know, walking his dog or something and he called to them...."

They were both silent, thinking about the escape.

"Here's my take," Carla finally said. "Let's do nothing. If he wants to call the law down on us, he will. If he wants to play cat and mouse, he'll do that. Or if he just wants to blow it off as a prank, he can do that, too. The ball is in his court."

"I have the note. He *did* write it."

"The confession? Disavowal, whatever you want to call it?"

"Plain and simple. In his handwriting."

"Well then," Carla said. "It worked. Did you bring it?"

"Nope. I stopped off at the cottage first. Now I've got to get rid of the ladder. I'd like to put it back but it's got fingerprints all over it.

"Just dump it in the bathtub with some detergent, that'll do it. Where'd you get it, anyway?"

"Borrowed it out of Conways' backyard, they've gone skiing over the break. The kids use it to get up to their tree house."

"Vance. Go home, wash the ladder, take it back, then

bring the note over here and let's put our heads together. Arthur can stay with me till you get back."

"If I don't get arrested in the meantime."

"You won't," Carla said. "We're going to come away clean."

XVIII

IT TOOK ALL MORNING to get Harold Baranoff's corpse out of the pit. Digger was sure it was a corpse they were dealing with, not an acutely ill, unconscious person. For one thing, he had observed no movement or sounds for the hour he squatted alongside the hole, waiting first for the state cops, then for the acting medical examiner, and finally, for the rescue squad to bring a ladder, rope, and an extra-strength canvas body bag. It was a bright sunny day, warming up significantly for mid-April; mockingbirds serenaded him during his long vigil. They sang cardinal songs offkey, imitated titmice and kinglets, and one made the approximate noises of semis on the highway.

Even though it would look unprofessional if they found him like this, Digger eventually gave in and sat down before the cops came, letting his legs dangle into the hole. Dr. Harold Baranoff, the Big Cheese, dead! Oh, there was going to be a scandal. An investigation, the mother of all investigations. He was too old and too fat for this kind of crisis. Theresa was right. He needed to cut down on sweets and get more exercise. If homicides were coming to plague Montandino, he also needed to think seriously about retirement.

The county's new Acting Med Ex, Laurence (with a u, please) Fasher, a trim and fussy young fellow in his forties, was wearing a white shirt and tie and plaid sports jacket. He replaced Henriette Fortenay, a large, stern woman with a mop of gray curls and cobalt blue eyes, who had held the post for as far back as Digger could remember.

Once you got to know Henriette, you saw that she was

precisely the right kind of person to make that clean cut from chin to pelvis an autopsy required. She could scoop out the organs as coolly as a skunk rolling eggs out of a bird's nest. And with the same dispassion. Nothing flummoxed, nothing displeased her. He'd seen her deal with one of Napara's crudest homicides, from a battered and ultimately carved up wife just last year to a freeway murder involving a .38. In the latter instance she was able to determine the trajectory of the bullet and from that to infer how closely the killer's car had drawn alongside and from that the state police were able to utilize several eyewitness accounts that narrowed the search to a Dodge Ram.

Now Henriette had retired and moved to San Diego where she could always see the ocean, and there was, Digger had gathered, some little wrangling about who should replace her. While this was being sorted out among the county commissioners, an Acting Medical Examiner had been appointed.

Digger sized this sporty fellow up as an out-of-stater and it turned out he was right. Fasher grew up in Missouri. He was a natural-born skeptic and he never let you forget it. Of course it went with the job, this doubting and inspecting. He doubted the subject could have fallen into the hole by accident. He doubted that the perpetrators could have carried him this far by hand, as it were. Fireman's carry, any old way at all. There was a vehicle, doubtless some mode of transport as yet undetermined. If he said, "I'm from Missouri," once, with a little deprecating laugh, he said it ten times before noon that day.

Fasher took forever fussing about how things should be done. He had his assistant take a hundred photos of the site, of the hole, of the general surroundings before they could even begin. He was not happy with the fact that Digger had sat down so casually at the scene; his buttocks on the earth may have obscured important evidence.

Rescue was finally allowed to put an aluminum exten-
sion ladder down. There wasn't room for two men to work
with the body, so they flipped a coin to see which one of
them would go. The burly one, a telephone lineman by trade,
won the toss. Once down there, he found cramming the
corpse into the canvas sack difficult. The body was *in rigor*,
Fasher's phrase, arms outflung. One leg lay bent under the
torso; the other stuck out sideways. The Rescue guy swore
a lot, sweating over his almost impossible assignment, and
Fasher leaned perilously above him barking orders. When
the rope was secured to the neck of the sack, Rescue climbed
out and extracted the ladder. Then he and his buddy and
Digger slowly pulled the dead man out of the pit. Fasher
stood, arms akimbo, supervising.

Then there was a little flareup over jurisdiction. The state
police wanted the lion's share. Digger had half a mind to
give the whole mess over to them and walk away, but this
was his town. This had happened on his watch; he had facts
and suppositions aplenty and he did not wish to divulge
them to these cocky youngsters who walked around in their
high leather boots as if they were Canadian Mounties.

All in all, it was noon before Digger got back to his office
and faced the onus of notifying next of kin. He was nervous, he was grieving, but above all, he was hungry. He
sent out for a ham and cheese on rye, double pickles, double
potato chips, and a large Diet Coke. And while he was waiting for his lunch to arrive he tried to figure out who to call
first.

Protocol dictated that he contact Baranoff's wife, but
when he dialed, only the disembodied voice of the Director
responded: "Hello. You have reached the home of Dr.
Harold Baranoff. No one is available to take your call just
now, but if you leave your name and number and the time

QUIT MONKS OR DIE! / 115

and date, we will get back to you as soon as possible." This was followed by a little cuckoo-cuckoo signal.

Digger heaved himself out of his chair; he'd have to go see for himself. As he traversed the broad, well-shaded streets of Montandino, all but deserted on a Monday noon, he tried to think how to pursue this case. Right off the cuff he could think of half a dozen people who would not be sorry to see Baranoff gone. Students, former students, possibly an old girlfriend or two. After that blowup at the Seder supper, his own twin brother had to be considered suspect. Even his wife and their two kids weren't above suspicion. Then there was Carla Strombaugh, certainly a possibility; she'd made no secret of her involvement with animal rights terrorists years ago when she was young and brash. And wasn't she a vegetarian? That alone signified something. He wished he had some info on The Mercy Bandits. They weren't local, he'd heard they were based somewhere in Utah, probably Carla had the facts. And then there were the Montandino shopkeepers who had had to deal with Baranoff's high-handed manner; he supposed he'd have to interview all the local merchants. Nobody liked the guy, but did that add up to wanting to rub him out?

There was no sign of life at the house. The garage doors were neatly closed, the expensive vertical blinds were drawn. The backyard looked freshly manicured. Nothing was out of place. He went back to the police car and dialed his own phone.

Digger frequently touched base with his wife throughout the day. Theresa, who knew the whereabouts of practically everyone in town, told him that Susie was away until tomorrow, earliest. The kids were staying with friends, and in any case he couldn't possibly tell them without an adult present. That left Baranoff's twin brother Vance. He decided to take a run up there, half hoping he wouldn't be home, either. He remembered during the war — World War II, the last good war was the way he thought of it — news of a death came by telegram. Or else it was two officers knocking at your door: Madam, I regret to inform you…. He supposed he could go get somebody from the county attorney's office to go with him. But they shouldn't be notified until there was evidence of a crime. He took a deep breath and once again turned the key in the ignition.

Vance came to the door so quickly that Digger had the eerie impression he'd been expected. He'd pretty much prepared his opening statement, but Vance preempted him.

"Hi, Digger. What's up? Want to come in?"

"Yes. Well. There's something I need to tell you."

"It's about Hal."

Digger was mildly surprised. But then he had read that twins had this special ability, that one somehow sensed what was happening with the other. He followed Vance into his study, noted that the computer was on and that there were three coffee cups lined up precariously on the pull-out shelf of the desk.

"Yes, it is about…Dr. Baranoff. I think you ought to sit down first."

Vance complied.

"I regret to tell you he's dead. Been found dead, about three hours ago."

"*Dead?*"

"I know this is a terrible shock. Your brother and all…."

"Where? Where'd you find him?"

"Well, you see there was a break-in. Two stolen monkeys…."

"He found them?"

"No. The custodian at the lab called me and I went over to investigate and…."

"You found them?"

"I found his body. In the monkey pit. The devil to get out." Digger thought he was saying it all wrong. He shouldn't be divulging information to a possible suspect. Not that *he* suspected him, but someone else might.

"But he can't be! In the pit, I mean. I mean, how did he get in there?"

"We're investigating that right now," Digger said, quite formally. "Chances are, whoever killed him knew about the pit and dumped his body in it."

"Whoever *killed* him? You're saying he was murdered?"

"We don't know that. But it's not likely that he just fell in. We won't know how he died until we get the medical examiner's report."

"When will that be?"

"Tomorrow, probably. Maybe later today. But in the meantime…."

"Does Susie know?"

"Nobody knows except you. I was going to ask you to help me notify the next of kin."

"Yes. Okay," Vance said. "Oh God. Susie's in San Francisco at her sister's, I can call her there, I guess. And the kids… Rachel's at Amanda's, they're probably both out at the stables. And Reuben, he's staying out at Joanna Hammerling's."

"I'll go with you," Digger said. "I'll wait while you call Mrs. Baranoff. Then Hammerling's first, I think. That way Reuben can come back with us to the stables."

"This will be hell for Rachel."

"Girls are always more emotional. I know, I have a daughter of my own," Digger said.

❒

Reuben was resetting some fence posts along the white

sand drive leading up to Joanna Hammerling's house. Digger admired the way the boy wielded the posthole digger; he'd had ample experience with one in his own youth. Reuben leaned on it for support while they told him his father was dead, possibly murdered. He swiped a shirtsleeve across his eyes.

"I better find Joanna," he said.

"I'll go with you," Vance offered.

Joanna Hammerling was magnificent, Vance thought. A take-charge woman with not a shred of self-doubt, she threw off her welding mask and rose from the ground, where she had been forming a joint between two massive tree limbs teased out of twisted steel.

She pulled Reuben to her fiercely and held him in a long embrace. "My poor darling," she said. "You just go along with your uncle and you call me. You hear, Reuben? You call me for any little thing, even just to talk."

"My car," he croaked.

"Don't you worry about your Beetle. It's safe right here. Nobody else is going to get behind the wheel."

He held out the posthole digger to Joanna, who accepted it solemnly. "You come to me, Reuben, I'm here for you." She gave him one more vise-tightening hug and then thrust him at Vance.

◌

Rachel had just finished bathing her horse and was scraping the excess water off his sides with an aluminum sweat scraper when Vance and Digger and Reuben pulled up in the Montandino police car. Vance saw her mouth go round with alarm; what was she anticipating?

Digger, for all his years of parenting, was awkward and tongue-tied. When Vance broke the news, Rachel paled visibly, gave a little animal cry of pain, and then stiffened. He knew she was holding something back, and he sensed that whatever it was, Reuben shared in the knowledge.

❐

"I think we ought to eat something," Vance said. He and the twins were sitting around the kitchen table; Susie was en route from San Francisco and Digger had gone to meet her plane.

"If I try to eat anything, I'll just throw up," Rachel said.

Reuben rummaged in the fridge and brought out some cheese, two tomatoes, and a jar of hot mustard. "Ray. Try to eat. Maybe not a sandwich. Maybe just some yogurt."

Vance silently fixed two sandwiches, hesitated, then fished out a beer. Why the hell not?

"I can't eat anything because it's just as though I killed him," Rachel said.

"Don't be ridiculous." Even as he said it Vance regretted the sharp edge in his voice.

"Well, you don't know, Uncle Vance. I *wished* him dead a thousand times."

Reuben said, "Ray. Wishing isn't the same as doing."

"'The thought is father to the deed,' Benny. Isn't that from Shakespeare or somebody?"

"'The wish is father to the thought,'" Vance said, rousing. "Shakespeare. But that isn't what he meant. It doesn't apply, Rachel."

❐

At last, when Susie came, there were tears. Vance found himself thinking that he had done more touching and holding in the last four hours than he had in four years. First, sitting between the twins in the back of Digger's squad car, he had kept one arm firmly around Rachel's shoulder to quiet her shivering. He thought of animals in the litter, how closely they press together for comfort. Well, they were his whole and entire family now, and he needed comfort, too. Now, embracing Susie, he was dangerously aware of her scent, the warmth and texture of her body as she grieved in his arms. He tried to will his penis into submission, but it awakened despite him as she pressed against him.

Digger stood tactfully off to one side, more chauffeur than Chief of Police. He had called Theresa again from the car, and she soon arrived with a casserole, a sponge cake and a quart of chocolate ice cream. Vance excused himself to call Carla, at Susie's request.

Digger and Theresa stayed for a decent interval. Theresa made a number of phone calls at Susie's direction. The newspapers were notified. Arrangements were made to have the body cremated as soon as it was released from the medical examiner's morgue. Susie thought a memorial service could be planned for later.

Much later, Vance thought. At a memorial service people get up and remember tender things about the deceased. It would be hard to find people with many tender memories of the late Director Baranoff.

Carla sat with the kids working a thousand-piece jigsaw puzzle she had thought to bring along. "The hardest thing in the world when there's a death," she said, "is how to pass the time. I remember when Marco was killed, all those hours waiting for the state to release the body, and then getting through the whole next day, and the next."

At nine o'clock Vance realized that he was dizzy from fatigue. Carla said she would spend the night with Susie and that he should go back to his cottage and pop a Valium or two. Vance agreed. More hugs all around; he was once again in peril with an erection.

◻

The twins went down the hall to their wing of the house. Susie opened a bottle of brandy Hal had bought for some occasion that had never taken place. It was aged brandy and they did not stint themselves.

"You know what this reminds me of?" Susie said.

"When your baby died."

"How did you know?"

"One death invites another," Carla said. "I've been reliving Marco's ever since I got here."

"You know, Hal never referred to Angela by name. I mean, we'd chosen the name together. Once, about a year after she died, we were walking past one of those little bodegas on Upper Broadway, and I stopped to admire this very pink and white infant in a carriage parked outside. I remember I said to him, 'Doesn't she remind you of Angela?'"

"And he said?"

"He said, 'Who?'"

Carla shook her head slowly.

"And why should he remember? He hadn't carried the baby fullterm. He hadn't panted and puffed through a ten-hour labor. His back rub— of course I had the misfortune to have back labor— his back rub was so perfunctory I had to beg the midwife to take over. Oh, he said some of the correct, calming things he'd learned in childbirth class, but after the baby finally was born he told me he'd been appalled at the quantity of blood and tissue involved. He'd thought it would be 'cleaner.' Cleaner!"

"Men," Carla said simply.

"Not all men," Susie said. "Theresa told me how terrific Digger was when Aurelia was born, how he asked to hold the baby and bathe her. Hal said he hadn't expected the umbilical cord to be a thick braid, or that you had to wash the waxy covering off the newborn. He said he hadn't realized how...primal the whole process was."

"But he was better about the twins, right?"

"I had to have a Caesarean three weeks early. My blood pressure was shooting up and the doctor was worried about eclampsia."

"You were lucky to have a doctor who knew the danger signs."

"Well, we spared Hal the ordeal that time, he was invited to watch the operation, but he doesn't...didn't...do well in the presence of blood."

"A lot of men can't stand the sight of real blood flowing."

Susie finished the brandy in her glass, then poured herself another two fingers. "When the twins were new, Hal hired a practical nurse to tend to them. I was supposed to stay in bed or at least on the sofa with my feet up for two weeks."

"Were you nursing?"

"You bet. Endlessly. Milk spurting all over the place the minute one of them mewed."

"He didn't like that?"

"Hal had as little to do with the babies as possible. I mean, he made faithful appearances, he admired them in their cribs. But he said they were too tiny for him to handle, too squirmy, too fragile."

"That figures."

"Later, he pretended he had a cold or was coming down with a cold, and for the longest time he managed always to be too importantly busy to change diapers or start the laundry. He was always willing to go fetch takeout food, though."

"Anything to get away from domestic responsibilities,"

Carla said.

"Well, he's away from them all now, isn't he?" Susie put down her glass and sobbed.

"It's okay," Carla soothed.

"Oh God, I'm so drunk. I don't know what I feel. Half grief, half relief. That's a poem."

IXX

"DAGO? Laurence Fasher here."

Digger grunted a response. It was six o'clock, Tuesday morning. He had lain awake half the night poring over the mysterious fact of Harold Baranoff's death and how it would reverberate in the community. Now here he was, the sleep-deprived Chief of Police, having to deal with this jacketed jerk who couldn't pronounce his name. An old Dick Gregory comedy routine flashed into his head, LBJ declaiming, "Nigger-oh, nigger-oh! Goddamn it, Lady Bird, I jest caint say it."

"Dago, you got a big problem over there. You got a major problem. This guy didn't die falling down the hole, he was already dead when he fell down. Or was pitched in. Also, I got news for you, he was nude when he died."

"Nude? How do you know?"

"His buttons were done up wrong, that's how. Must've been hard work stuffing him back in his clothes. Even a body that isn't in rigor is hard as hell to dress."

"When do you figure...?"

"T.o.d.? I fix the time of death at around 6, 8 p.m. Sunday."

"6, 8 p.m. Sunday," Digger repeated, mentally running the day backward. "You're sure?"

"Look at it this way, Dago. The body is in rigor, fresh as a daisy, the flesh blanches when I press different parts of it. That says it's dead less than eight to twelve hours. Blood settles along gravitational lines so it looks almost like a bruise, blanching on the pressure points. Where he landed, capiche?"

"Go on."

"Okay. Then I check the eyes. When I pull the lids back I see that the cornea is still crystal clear. That tells me the body has been there less than twenty-four hours. So we're still talking Sunday, Sunday night, some time before midnight."

"Okay. Anything else?"

"About the body. What you've got here, Dago, is a bit of a nasty. Never mind the brush abrasions from hitting the sides of the pit as he fell in. This guy has a blush of erythema around his neck that goes straight across. This tells me he was strangled, probably with a soft scarf or cotton tee shirt. Also, petechiae, little burst blood vessels, on the sclera of the eyes, that's consistent with strangulation."

"You mean he strangled himself?"

"He could have done it himself, but I doubt it. We see that in teenage boys who like to half-hang themselves while they masturbate. Vagal inhibition. It prolongs orgasm, you see."

"But you don't think...."

"Not in his case. In his case it was done by somebody else. There's abrasions around both wrists, looks like he was tied up, most likely handcuffed."

"And struggled to get loose?"

"Exactly. Also, I can tell you the subject ejaculated before he died."

"So what are you saying?"

"I'm saying what you got here, Dago, is a big-city thing, a kinky S & M thing."

"You're saying he died having some sort of weirdo sex?"

"Weirdo's a matter of taste. I'm saying he died during, or immediately after. Possibly precipitated by a heart attack. I'll have to do an autopsy."

Digger exhaled noisily. "Jesus, Mary and Joseph."

"I don't envy you, Dago, dealing with the family and all. The pillar of the community, though from what I hear, a lot of folks disliked him. But there's one more thing."

"I'm listening."

"I personally went down in the hole yesterday afternoon to see for myself. And what I found down there is a puzzle, Dago."

"What?"

"Human excrement, that's what. Also, traces of urine in the soil."

"Whose?"

"Good question. Somebody was down there long enough to produce these wastes. I can tell you, Dago, this isn't new shit. It's two, three days old."

Digger didn't have the heart to ask Fasher how he knew this. "But couldn't somebody else just have come along and, you know, used the hole for a latrine?"

"Doubt it. My take on it is somebody was down there for a while and maybe not by choice, you follow?"

Digger followed. "You know this was an isolation pit for monkeys."

"We're not talking monkeys here, Dago. Now what I'd like for you to do is swear out a warrant for me and you to look over the deceased's clothes closet and such, say, in an hour. His bedroom, his bathroom, that sort of thing."

"A search warrant."

"Well, Dago, that's what the Chief of Police does, right?"

"Meet you there at nine o'clock," Digger said curtly, and hung up the phone.

❒

Susie said she wanted to be present at the inspection. She was dry-eyed and withdrawn, but alert to every nuance. She had not, she said, re-entered their bedroom on the supposition that the police would want to look there for evidence. She had not entered the master bath, for the same reason. She had called Carla, who came and spent the night with her. They'd sat up talking in the kitchen until two o'clock; then they'd catnapped in the family room on twin studio couches.

There was nothing untoward in the living room or kitchen. Fasher declined Susie's offer of coffee and a muffin. Digger, although his stomach was growling with hunger pangs, felt constrained to do the same. The trio went through the connecting door into the capacious three-car garage, its back wall lined with storage cabinets.

Susie thought to herself how much of a family's history resides in what is outgrown but not discarded: Rachel's eighth grade science project, a plaster of Paris bas relief of the coast of northern California; Reuben's bow and arrow set from his tenth birthday; a cardboard carton of old snapshots; their wedding album; two mess kits; a Columbia University reunion umbrella; a pair of hockey ice skates, and a handsewn crib-size quilt. This she unfolded and refolded, choking back a sob. Digger clucked his sympathy. But why did this item evoke tears?

"It was Angela's, the baby we lost," Susie said. "I worked on this all through my pregnancy. See the rabbits?" She managed a wan smile.

Along the far wall, Digger and Fasher discovered a black plastic leaf bag that had been stuffed into a trash barrel. It contained a stained, wet jacket Susie identified as one Hal frequently wore to the lab. A filthy pair of chinos, wadded up boxer shorts, a pale blue broadcloth shirt with button-down collar. Socks and mud-caked loafers. She couldn't swear these were the garments he was wearing last Friday, but it seemed likely. The three of them stood rooted in the garage musing over the collection of clothing until, almost as an afterthought, Susie pointed out to them that the BMW was missing.

Upstairs, the master bathroom bore signs of a recent shower. Fasher collected two black hairs from the tile floor. He took the bath towel, the electric razor lying on the sink counter, and the Dior aftershave as well. He snooped, but in a disinterested fashion, through the drawers of Hal's bureau and the nightstand drawer on Hal's side of the bed. He methodically inspected the contents of Hal's closet, fishing through every pocket of Hal's sizeable collection of suit and sports jackets. From the inner vest pocket of a coffee-colored corduroy jacket he drew forth a folded sheet of paper.

It was a painstakingly assembled note composed of individual letters cut out of magazines and pasted up to form a sentence. Fasher smoothed it out and laid it on the bed, where he, Digger and Susie could read it together.

QUIT MONKS OR DIE!

"Any idea who?" he asked Susie. She shook her head.

"Dago?"

"Could be one of those liberation fronts. You know, like The Mercy Bandits?"

"Never heard of them."

"They're an interventionist animal rights group," Susie said. "They break into labs, destroy records, that sort of thing. Acts of civil disobedience."

"You know any of these people?"

"No. Not personally. I've heard about them and read about them."

"Heard from who?"

Susie wasn't going to say; Digger knew she was thinking *Carla*.

"I'll take that note," Digger said, extending his hand for it.

Fasher drew back.

"It's a police matter," Digger said. "Nothing to do with the medical examiner's office."

Fasher handed it over reluctantly. "Talk to you later, Dago," he said as he hefted his trash bag.

After Fasher had gone, Susie said, "I knew about that note."

"You did? When?"

"Oh, a couple of weeks ago. He showed it to me."

"What did he say?"

"Not much. He made a joke about it, said every murder mystery he'd ever read had a threatening note disguised that way."

"Did he say who he thought...?"

"He said it was a copycat thing, crudely put together. 'Just a little offering from The Mercy Bandits,' was the way he put it. He said, 'They talk the talk but they're about as threatening as...Vance's spotted dog.'"

XX

DIGGER SAT IN HIS OFFICE Wednesday morning glumly nibbling a low-fat granola bar in place of his two sugared doughnuts and sipping his extra-large coffee diluted with skim milk instead of his usual half and half. These deprivations did not help him to fit the pieces of the Baranoff murder puzzle together, but he supposed that some poor nourishment was better than total abstinence.

Dr. Baranoff's 1999 model BMW had turned up late yesterday at the mouth of the canyon, neatly parked and unlocked. The keys were not in their usual place atop the sun visor on the driver's side; in fact, one of the puzzles, Hal's intact keychain, had been found lying on the front hall table of the house.

Whoever had stolen the BMW hadn't abandoned it in haste. Digger had already had it dusted for fingerprints, but as he suspected, there were none.

So whoever killed him took his keys and...drove the car to the canyon? If so, how did the whole keychain get back in the house? Or say the perpetrator intercepted him at the foot of the canyon, returned the keys to the house and then carted him off to the pit in a separate car. Why?

Who sent the note? Had it been mailed to the Director or had it come in the office mail?

Why the strangle marks and wrist abrasions on the body? If inflicted in somebody's bed, whose?

And how did the dead body — presuming it was dead by then — get from point X to the monkey pit?

His stomach was rumbling, chewing over these indigestible pieces. Well, it was probably best to start with the car.

Why was it abandoned at the mouth of the canyon?

He sighed and dialed Theresa. She praised him for sticking to his diet and scolded him for not finding out that Dr. Baranoff had leased a cabin in the canyon from a retired professor at the Theological School. It was common knowledge in Montandino; everybody knew Dr. B. was a rock jock, a heavy hiker, a regular Boy Scout.

After he got off the phone with Theresa, Digger called Laurence (with a u, please) Fasher. He was in for it, all right. The damned cabin was way the hell up the gorge and the only way to get to it was either on horseback or by shank's mare. If the murder had taken place in the cabin, Fasher stood to collect some vital evidence. If not, well, Digger was in purgatory. Horses were out of the question. He was consigned to undertake a two- or three-hour rocky climb with a man who couldn't, or wouldn't, pronounce a simple Latino name.

When they met at the parking strip, Digger, who was still in official uniform, saw that Fasher had substituted a natty nylon windbreaker for his sport coat and high-top sneakers for his loafers. Moreover, he was wearing a backpack.

"Standard sleuthing equipment," he said. "Also, water, and some fruit. We might need it, Dago. It's heating up to be a good one."

Two-and-a-half arduous hours later, sweating profusely, Digger hauled himself onto the deck of the cabin. His feet hurt and he was starving. They had stopped twice; once, to peel and eat two oranges, and next, to take a piss and drink some water. And to think people did this every weekend for fun!

Fasher, who had long since taken off his windbreaker and tied it around his waist, was slightly damp and in excellent spirits. "Gorgeous country, Dago. I tell you, I had no idea, no idea at all you had hills like these."

"Foothills," Digger managed to say. He fingered the pad-lock on the front door. "I guess we gotta break in."

"Let me case the joint first," Fasher said merrily, and dis-appeared around the corner of the building.

Digger sat down on the top step, leaned his head against the support post of the railing and hoped it would take the Med Ex a while. He also hoped he'd be able to get up again.

Fasher, who had jimmied open a back window, reap-peared after a decent interval. "Nothing," he said. "The place is as clean as a whistle, no dropped hankies or underpants. Not so much as a stray toothpick. I took the precaution of dusting for fingerprints."

"But if it isn't a criminal whose prints are already on file...," Digger said.

"We're cooked," Fasher agreed. "But what a day! Wasn't it a lovely climb?"

By the time Digger got back to his office, the whole day was cooked. There was still the unsolved riddle of who had driven the BMW. The keychain on the front hall table. The Quit Monks note. The strangle marks. Etcetera, etcetera. He took another low-fat granola bar out of his desk and tried to imagine it into a Baby Ruth.

XXI

GREAT FRESHETS of rain slashed through the canyon all day Saturday. Fifi had awakened several times during the night to hear its pelting force but each time drifted back into the deep sleep of someone safely encased in a cocoon. When she finally rose, layered on another sweater and remade the fire, it was midmorning.

Wherever Hal was, she wished him well. She was pretty sure he hadn't had an accident climbing the canyon; it was more likely that he never left Montandino. Something, anything could have come up at the last minute. There might have been a family emergency involving a broken arm, a traffic accident, Susie might have returned unexpectedly so that he couldn't get away. Well, she would sit out the rainstorm, enjoy a murder mystery or two— the cabin was richly endowed with Dick Francis and P.D. James— and if it cleared sufficiently, trudge back down later today.

The front didn't move out until dusk. Felicity uncorked a lovely bottle of Pinot Noir, opened a tin of smoked oysters and gave herself over to gustatory pleasure. Again, she slept the sleep of the entirely innocent, snug and untroubled as a small child in a loving home. She was up at first light on Sunday, breakfasted and tidied the cabin, careful to restow every article she had unpacked. At 6 a.m. she went out the door.

The hike down progressed swiftly in the chilly morning air. As the sun rose, everything sparkled with miniature rainbows, as if in salute to Easter. The ground squirrels were active, some unseen birds called and called, the gravelly scree scrunched and slid rhythmically under her confident footsteps.

There were exactly three vehicles in the parking area at the canyon base, hers, a BMW drawn alongside her Honda, and an old black pickup truck that probably belonged to one of the park's maintenance workers. But if the BMW was Hal's...she felt a sudden stab of fear. It was his, all right. The vertical scratch along the front right fender had been inflicted by a malevolent child's bicycle chain. A dancing monkey medallion hung from the rearview mirror.

Terror now overtook her. So he *had* come to the canyon, he *had* tried to reach her. He might even have started hiking up, slipped, fallen, broken a hip, fractured his skull.... Somehow she couldn't visualize Hal in any of those predicaments. No, he must have met someone here, been deflected from starting out.

She thought about notifying the authorities — wasn't that the phrase they used? But to do so would call attention to her own presence on the mountain. She might even be implicated in some way. She had to think about her own future, after all. She was an only child; her father, who had decamped when she was three, was a ghost in a tweed jacket with big pockets, out of which came sticks of gum and jelly beans. From as far back as Felicity could remember, her mother had been office manager for J. C. Goodnow in New Haven. And while they lived quietly but decently on her salary, down the line, Felicity knew, she'd have her mother to look after.

Her entire future depended on this relationship with Hal, on this grad school stipend he had obtained for her. To look that future square in the face as a single, self-supporting young woman deprived of her position at the lab... well, she supposed there were other avenues. Other institutions that would want her. But what if there were no jobs? Things were tight in academia unless you were some interesting ethnic minority. She could always hire out as a cocktail waitress, an upscale restaurant hostess, a secretarial temp.

Oh God, but what about Hal? Maybe he'd been kidnapped by some animal rights terrorist group like The Mercy Bandits. Hal thought she didn't know anything about his primate experiments, but she wasn't as naive as she let on. And anyway, after the *Clarion* article, almost everyone in town knew about his pit of despair. She had a pretty good idea of where it was, too.

It was hard work alternating roles with Hal, playing the intelligent, responsive yet submissive graduate student by day and the harsh dominatrix by night. When Hal prepared a paper for publication, Felicity handled the footnotes and bibliography. She checked his citations for accuracy and the text for typos. She faxed, she collated, she kept checklists of other behaviorists' experiments and made précises of them for Hal to look over.

As his graduate assistant she had to soothe and cajole, massage egos and be on call. As his mistress she was supposed to be threatening, punishing, dangerous. She dressed in leather, she dressed in medical whites. She had a rubber cat suit Hal especially liked. With it she wore platform high-heeled boots and carried a riding crop.

Actually, she found acting out her daytime part more degrading than being a dominatrix. Sadomasochistic sex play was only a game. Behavioral psych was the gateway to a career.

The first thing to do, she told herself, was to drive back to Montandino and check out his house. Maybe there was a message there, a clue to his whereabouts. She lifted the keychain, complete with house and Graysmith Lab keys, from the BMW's visor and tucked them into her backpack. On second thought, she also took the garage door opener from the dashboard cubbyhole.

It was still early enough so that nothing was stirring in town. The street in front of Baranoffs' house was deserted; she drove cautiously to the end of the block, then circled back. Using Hal's automatic garage door opener, she slipped the Honda inside and reclosed the door.

Nothing was amiss in the house, nothing untoward in his study or the family room. No notes, no clues. The kitchen was spotless. A lone plate with bread crumbs and a coffee mug stood in the sink. It made her flesh creep, tiptoeing around in here. She swiftly exited the way she had come, drove to the lab and pulled the Honda all the way around back behind the service fence, where it would be out of sight of any custodians coming by to tend the monkeys she knew were sequestered on the forbidden third floor. Then she set out on foot for the pit.

There wasn't any path to follow. Rather, there were multiple paths striking out in the chaparral this way and that, possibly deer paths. Any one of them could be the right one. It was like trying to thread your way through a maze, Felicity thought, tramping between creosote bushes and minor cactus plants. Probably there was a back way in to the pit, too, across what looked like half a mile of scrub growth, probably full of poisonous snakes and God knows what other reptiles.

When she came to the pit, she heard him calling Help! in the same piteous tones he used in certain scenarios in bed. She dislodged the grating and yanked the plywood free.

"Jesus! That *is* you!"

"You're damned right it's me," Hal said. "I've been yelling and yelling ever since I heard footsteps. Somehow you've got to get me out of here."

"Should I go back and call 911?"

"No! Christ Almighty, I don't want anybody to know

I'm down here."

"Hal. Who did this?"

"Never mind that. Got your backpack with you?"

"I'm wearing it."

"Got the Swiss Army knife I gave you?"

She fished around for it.

"Drop it down."

He tugged it open, grunted, and set to work cutting long strips of his sleeping bag ground sheet and poncho. They didn't speak as he knotted these together.

"All right. Stand back. I'm going to throw this rope up to you. It'll probably take me a couple of tries."

"Shit." The coil approached the lip of the pit and fell back into the hole.

"Fifi! Lie down on the edge and try to grab it when it comes close."

Terrified of toppling in, on the fifth try she was nevertheless able to catch hold of the slimy mass.

"Can you find something to tie it to?"

There was a small tree nearby, she thought it was some sort of oak. "It's pretty skinny. I don't know if it'll hold," she called down to him.

"Well, get behind it, wrap your arms around it and try to brace it. I'm coming up."

In a few minutes he was standing beside her, wet and dishevelled, blinking like a bat in the sunlight.

"Who *did* this to you?" she asked again.

"Never mind, I'll tell you later. Let's get the fuck out of here."

They drove back to Hal's house, and Felicity once again pulled the little Honda into the garage. "Where'd you get the opener? And my house keys? Smart girl."

"Out of your car. It's parked at the canyon."

"Sonofabitch," he said. While Felicity opened the door

between the garage and the kitchen, Hal stripped and stuffed his clothes into one of the black plastic leaf bags stored on the back shelf. He went shivering upstairs for a long, hot shower, came down freshly shaven, redolent of Dior, and in clean clothes. With a flourish he placed his keyring on the front hall table.

"Where are we going?" Felicity asked him.

"Your place. You're going to cook me a big fat breakfast."

XXII

WEDNESDAY NIGHT Digger reclined in the bathtub into which Theresa had emptied an entire box of baking soda.

"It draws out the pain," she told him. "You just soak there a while and when you get out, you'll see. You'll be as good as new."

"As good as old," Digger groaned. Every muscle in his body throbbed. He turned on the hot water tap again and tried to map out a strategy. Two strategies, really. One to solve the murder, and the other to keep the lurid details out of the hands of the media. He could just see QUIT MONKS OR DIE! blazoned across the front page of any one of southern California's tabloids. It would be hell for Susie and the kids. It would be very bad for the Graysmith reputation. And now that Fasher had seen the note, how far could he trust Fasher?

So far, there had been only a sober obituary notice and a feature news item about Graysmith, its eminent Director, and Montandino as the little town that was still living in the thirties. Dr. Harold Baranoff's career, his insightful direction of the now world-renowned Graysmith Laboratory, got the most play. The article focused on Graysmith's pioneering studies in early childhood development. Baranoff's death was listed as "an unfortunate accident."

"When asked if foul play was suspected, Chief Martinez replied, 'We haven't entirely ruled it out.'" Nothing yet about the monkey subjects, the drowned infant, the catatonic mother, the dangerous biters who had been experimented upon. Nothing about the theft of the squirrel monkey pair. It was a miracle that the inquiring reporter hadn't

connected with the *Clarion* editorial denouncing the deprivation experiments. But how long could Digger hold off
the hounds? And for that matter, how long before the dis-
trict attorney's office made its move? Fasher was just the
kind of loose cannon who would decide this was a kidnapping and insist that the D.A. call in the FBI.

"When Mark Twain wanted to get rid of a character,"
Fasher told him as they came out of the canyon to their
cars, "he just dropped him down the well. He did it twice,
in fact. *Pudd'nhead Wilson*, that's the book."

Digger, who had never read any Mark Twain, grunted.

"See you in the funny papers, Dago."

❐

Digger made a mental list of all possible suspects:

Manuel? He was a deep one, that compadre, an honor-
able man without a drop of malice in his veins. Still, he was
underpaid and overworked, he received no recognition
within the lab. Certainly he didn't like Baranoff. But did he
dislike him enough to want to do away with him?

Joanna Hammerling? Well, she was out of the
Montandino loop, but she adored Reuben. She would lay
down her life for that boy; why not his father's life if she
thought he was in the way?

The Graysmith graduate students? They were at the
moment faceless, though he knew there was a pert redheaded female among them. He'd seen her downtown half
a dozen times, sometimes with a guy who looked as though
he could play tight end for the Packers. He'd have to look
into that. Any grad student of the Director's might have a
good reason to want him gone.

And then there was Drew Deveraux, who used to work
at Graysmith, and whose mother had played nursemaid to

the twins until her final nervous breakdown. He still cased the town, cruising. Digger remembered he had seen his truck Easter Sunday morning. Theresa said he had cancer and that it was terminal. Poor bastard, life had handed him a pretty raw deal.

Carla Strombaugh. Although she'd been clean now for several years, she had a lengthy arrest record for terrorist acts, destroying records in research labs that tested and killed minks, mice, rabbits and so on. She'd been part of some Greenpeace actions, she freely admitted she'd had friends in The Mercy Bandits. It was likely she'd been a member at some point.

And The Mercy Bandits themselves needed to be considered. An undercurrent of admiration for the Bandits' acts often rippled through the community. Abused horses seemed to invite intervention by women, Digger mused. For that matter, abused animals in general. Well, The Mercy Bandits were an underground organization with tentacles that stretched in every direction. They were terrorists; they were proud to be terrorists. If they were involved in Baranoff's murder, the connection would have to be through Carla.

Baranoff's twin brother Vance. The Director had brought him out here from back east in the first place; Digger thought it was more to lord it over him than out of family feeling. They were an unlikely pair, those two. No love lost between them. In fact, he'd seen Dr. B. throw an adult-sized tantrum when Vance provoked him. And Vance could give it back, too. "We're fraternal twins," Vance was at pains to point out. "Two eggs, two separate sacs, even if we do look alike."

True, despite the resemblance, no one with his wits about him could mistake one for the other. Reuben and Rachel were fraternal twins, too. Reuben had given Digger a little lecture on the subject once. "In the case of Siamese twins,"

Reuben had said, "if one is lefthanded, the other will be righthanded. If one twin's heart is on the left, the other's has to be on the right. They're mirror images of each other. We're just brother and sister who happened to be born at the same time." Yes, it could well have been Vance. Maybe Vance *and* Carla together.

It was a short list, after all.

XXIII

WIND CHIMES on the cabin's porch were tinkling noisily, relentlessly and he meanwhile was still climbing toward them. His legs were stone pillars. Each step that he took required immense effort, but even so he wasn't narrowing the distance. As Digger reached out his hand to still the insistent metallic clatter, his fingers closed on the telephone. Groggily, hauling himself up on one elbow, he picked up the receiver.

"Is this? Is this the Chief of Police?"

The digital clock on the bureau winked 3:47.

"Who's calling?"

"Oh dear. I think I waked you up, I'm sorry. First I called the New York State Police and they told me to call the California State Police and they finally gave me your name but not your number and then they hung up and when I called them back no one would answer, so then I called Information and they gave me your number."

Digger sighed deeply. It was too early to have to deal with a distraught woman. "What is this in regard to?"

"My daughter. My daughter Felicity Shugrue. I keep calling her house and getting the answering machine, I don't know where she is or why she hasn't called me back. It isn't like her, it isn't like her at all, we talk every Monday and Thursday morning at six o'clock sharp her time, we're both larks and it's easy for us to talk first thing in the morning, and last Thursday she told me she was going hiking in a famous canyon over the Easter holiday but she'd talk to me Monday like always, and I haven't heard a word from her and I don't know another soul out there I can ask where she's gone."

Digger held the receiver away from his ear. The disembodied voice kept on.

"so finally I thought, the police, the police will go out there and see if she's home or if she got lost on the hiking trip, I just didn't know what else to do...."

By now Digger was fully awake; he reached for his notepad and pen and took down Felicity Shugrue's mother's name and address, her phone number in New Haven, Connecticut, her daughter's approximate height, weight, hair and eye color. Her daughter's address and phone number in the valley.

"Yes. Okay, I know where that is. Any particular friends she mentions? Did she say who else was going on this hike?"

"No. No, she doesn't say much about the people at the lab. There's someone named Rick she sometimes goes out with, she says he's just a friend, but I don't even know his last name."

That would be the guy who looked like a player on the Packers; presumably, he was a grad student, too.

"I'll tell you what, Mrs. ...Shugrue," Digger said. "I'll take a run out there and make sure she's okay. Chances are she's staying with some friends nearby, maybe they got to partying up there in the canyon and haven't come down yet. There's almost always a logical explanation."

But his antennae told him something was up. Theresa made him sit down and eat a sensible breakfast before he dressed, pulled on his boots, strapped on his holster and settled his official police hat on his head. She made him wait until the sky was showing some pale streaks in the east and then she stood in the doorway and watched him back the cruiser out and turn onto the blacktop.

Felicity Shugrue of New Haven, Connecticut, and Rick Whoever-he-was, Digger said to himself as if he were repeating a mantra. He supposed they were lovers in the casual way young people nowadays entered into, what did they call them? relationships. He guessed they had lit out for a couple of days in Mexico over the Easter break, downed too much tequila, and were sleeping it off in some sleazy motel south of the border. He doubted that his trip out to the valley would turn up anything more than an empty house.

This Felicity would be roughly the same age as his Aurelia, who was now a flight attendant and travelled all over the world. He and Theresa had guarded their daughter like hungry watchdogs when she was little. He supposed this Mrs. Shugrue had done the same. He supposed that growing up in New Haven was a lot more dangerous than in Montandino. Probably this Felicity knew how to handle herself in the big city, probably she was bored to death out here in the desert with no night life and no fancy restaurants and that was why she had gone off with this Rick Whoever for a little excitement across the Rio Grande.

He followed the gentle curve of the gravel driveway up to the medievalists' house. The front door was locked; slowly, he eased himself around to the back and stood for a moment on the porch. The perfume from the wisteria made him sneeze. He struggled to get his handkerchief out of his hip pocket, then blew his nose loudly. After he stuffed the handkerchief back, he tried the door. It opened at his touch.

There was blood everywhere, and an overpowering stench. Felicity Shugrue's decaying body lay face down on the kitchen floor. The cats had obviously feasted on what they could lap up. There was no sign of forced entry; no smashed crockery or overturned furniture.

Fasher will love this one, Digger thought grimly. This one calls for the crime lab, the whole nine yards. He went back out to the cruiser and placed his call. There was a small distinct pleasure in catching the Acting Medical Examiner asleep in his bed.

XXIV

*I WAS DREAMING MA. I always called her Ma. Ma, I said, goddamnit,
you're drunk again, passed out cold again, pissing the bed again*

❒

*and then I was remembering when we lived in Billings and you
were a bookkeeper for Allied Holdings and I played shortstop on the
high school team, Drew Deveraux, freshman shortstop, you've gotta
be small and fast for that with trigger reflexes, that's what made me
such a good bronc rider when I dropped out of eleventh grade and
after I had broke six ribs and stuck one through my left lung and
couldn't do the rodeos no more I was a damn decent cowpuncher*

❒

*and you dried out and stayed sober for months at a time and I got
happy with some money in my jeans and a safe home to come back
to nights*

❒

*until always there'd be another binge, I couldn't stand it, there
wasn't any steady man, just a parade of sadasses you'd latched onto
to get you through the lonely nights. I never met my father if you
even knew who he was, I left for good forever after waking up to some
strange guy in his underwear blowing his nose in the kitchen only it
wasn't forever, I kept coming back the way you kept sobering up*

❒

and every time that you stayed sober you'd start in dreaming of California, someplace warm to heal the ulcers on your legs, California, land of golden opportunity, I never

☐

found the wife there you were after me to find, truth is, I never told you, I didn't care for women

☐

you were the only woman, the good mother, when you were one

☐

you'd be surprised what cowboys do with other cowboys

☐

you were my safe place even though I was the one that did the looking after

☐

and then you got a nanny job, you loved it

☐

the kids called you Lottie-dear, they made you a member of the family, I stayed away from that as long as you were dry, I was 30, you were 50, we joked we'd have another 50

☐

I got to where my body was so sore from all the pounding in the saddle that I couldn't work the cattle drives, He gave me a job too at the lab he ran

❐

He was decent to you, paid your detox at that place called The Open Door which was a lie, the doors were double locked no visitors for Lottie Deveraux the first six weeks, you came back looking plump and pink, She said it was heaven having you come back so healthy, He gave that fake smile He always put on when He thought He ought to, He knew there was no cure for what you had

❐

no cure for what I have, you didn't give me cancer with your drinking, no you didn't, He was decent to you till you hit the skids the next time, then they put you in a mental hospital, they said you drank because of your depression, your agitation and depression and confusion, it goes the other way around, why can't they see it, She went to visit you and brought you flowers, you drank the bottle of cologne She gave you

❐

after that it was a halfway house in L.A., I could have told them it was halfway to the bottom, to begging on the main streets, bag lady with a shopping cart till you OD'd on an access road beside the freeway

❐

half a mile from the halfway house in L.A.

She went with me into the morgue to say it really was you

□

I don't blame them, they were decent to you

□

Ma, you were a sorry piece of work, they were so sorry, everybody was so sorry

□

and now the story's ended

XXV

EVEN THOUGH it had taken place twenty miles out of town, news of the murder stunned Montandino. The state police hauled the cats away to the local shelter, the forensic team dusted everything for fingerprints. It didn't take a brain surgeon to see that Felicity Shugrue had died of a vicious stab wound, but Laurence Fasher took possession of the body to determine cause and method of death.

"Right through the chest wall," Fasher said. "Instant. Or pretty close to instant."

The murder weapon was lying on the floor beside the body, a Williams Sonoma carving knife, the kind commonly found in butcher block holders in the kitchens of the affluent.

"A crime of passion," he said. "It seems the murderer was too carried away to conceal his weapon."

"Or her," said Digger.

"Her?"

"Weapon. The knife. What makes you think the killer was a man?"

"Well, Dago, when you find a young woman who has bled to death on the kitchen floor the murderer is usually... her lover."

"Let's not jump the gun," Digger said. "In a manner of speaking."

Fasher arranged for the body's removal to the county morgue. The lab crew packed up its equipment. Digger lingered for a long time at the site. Who was this Felicity? Who were her enemies?

XXVI

W<small>HEN</small> M<small>ANUEL</small> A<small>GOSTA</small> heard the news of Dr. Baranoff's demise, he had to admit that what he felt was relief. No more separations, no more terror in the monkey house. The Graysmith comptroller— there was no Assistant Director, not since last year when the man who held that position had resigned—came up himself to tell Manuel that Harold Baranoff had met his death in an unfortunate accident. The experiments were henceforth cancelled, the monkeys were to be rehabilitated and returned to some not yet designated appropriate agency. Manuel was now in full charge.

The first thing Manuel did was to unshackle the cages from one another so that they could be moved from place to place. He aligned #2 alongside #4, two young females he thought would get along. After socializing them face to face for a few days he thought he could risk putting them in together. If that worked, he would try others in that way.

From the playschool downstairs he cadged some outworn toys, rattles, plastic mirrors and doughnut posts on which variously colored rings were meant to fit. In the past he had been expressly forbidden to provide his subjects with any mental or physical stimulation; now he went outside and picked a basket of withered oranges from the ornamental trees that grew everywhere in Montandino. Much bewildered excited chittering took place as he distributed the toys and orange halves.

He wasn't terribly surprised to receive a visit from Dr. Baranoff's daughter. Pale and subdued as a beaten animal, she brightened considerably when she saw his new arrangements. They walked the length of the room together. The place was alive with the noise of chattering macaques. Now the cages faced one another. Monkeys reached between the bars to touch one another. Some were beginning to hand rattles and mirrors back and forth.

"Did you come alone?"

"Yes."

"Are you all right, mi nina?"

"I came to confess something, Manuel."

"I already know, mi quereda."

"What do you already know? Who told you?"

"That you stole the little monkeys? No one had to tell me."

"And you're not...? You didn't...?"

"I didn't tell. I was relieved to find them missing. I will never tell. Now you must keep them warm. In the winter they must come inside, they will need their shots twice a year. You will find a good monkey doctor?"

"I will, Manuel. What will happen to these?"

"The experiments are over. We will try to make them back into normal monkeys now. Then they will go somewhere, somewhere perhaps on an island of other monkeys—" here he knew he was embroidering for her sake— "and they will have new lives."

"Did you know that I stole your keys?"

"I had new ones made, mi piquena."

"I'm sorry if I got you into trouble."

"That was no trouble. That was justice."

He thought perhaps she stood a little straighter walking out.

❒

Vance came to supper at Susie's on Wednesday and again on Thursday. Susie went over to Carla's for several hours on Wednesday to get away from the incessant ringing of the phone, the arrival of assorted curiosity seekers and the delivery of messages and flowers. On Thursday her sister Liz flew in from San Francisco. Reuben had come home reluctantly from Joanna Hammerling's; Joanna had insisted, saying the family needed him.

"You mean I'm the man of the family now?"

"I know you're hurting. But Rachel needs you, your mother needs you, too."

"Christ. I wish I were out of all this. Out on some desert island."

"It's going to get a lot more unpleasant," Joanna told him. "Your father was murdered. Whoever did it must have had a reason."

"A lot of people had reasons. A lot of people really hated him."

"It could have been a blackmail plot that backfired," Joanna said. "Or something to do with his experiments, it could have been some deranged person, an ex-student."

"Or a terrorist group?"

"Possibly."

"The hard thing is, I can't think of a single person who really *liked* him."

"You did, Reuben. You and Rachel did."

He chose not to dispute her.

Vance had made spaghetti with sauce and a big tossed salad. He had insisted that Susie take Liz over to Carla's, where they could have some quiet time together. Susie thought she might cook dinner for the three of them there.

"Something vegan, it's a challenge."

"Not as hard as it sounds," Vance said. "Carla is entirely normal in her own way."

"Even if she only eats plants," Susie managed a small smile.

Reuben ate heartily, his first real meal since the…what did he call it to himself? The murder. He would have to get used to his father's murder.

Rachel picked at her portion.

"Ray, if you don't start eating pretty soon, you're going to fade away," Reuben said.

"Maybe that's what I ought to do. Maybe that's what I want to happen."

"Why, Rachel? Why do you keep blaming yourself?" Vance asked.

"Because I practically killed him off myself. I was the one who sent that QUIT MONKS note. I sat in my bedroom and cut those letters out of old magazines and pasted them up and put it in Daddy's office mail two weeks ago."

Vance clucked and shook his head. A ghost of a smile played about his mouth.

"Ray, I think we better tell Uncle Vance about the squirrel monkeys, too."

"We stole them Sunday night, we've got them hidden out at Joanna's."

"She doesn't know they're there," Reuben said hastily. "We've got them hidden way out in an old barn."

"I just couldn't let Daddy take her baby away from her, she's so little. So…helpless."

"Well, don't waste time feeling guilty about that," Vance said. "I'd have done the same thing, so would Carla. So would almost anybody if they'd known how to."

Rachel sighed an oceanic sigh. Sudden tears came to her eyes.

"You know, you're allowed to feel sad," Vance said gently. "You're allowed to remember some good things about your father, things that make you miss him. Because you kids did love him, in spite of everything."

"And what about you?" Reuben asked. "You're his twin.

Did you love him, too?"

Vance was silent. Did he? Somewhere down deep in his atavism he missed his rotten brother. Pitied and loathed him and yes, even deeper than that pulsed the blood connection that said love.

"I did. He was my other self."

XXVII

It was almost noon on Thursday when Digger knocked on Vance's front door. Arthur came around the corner of the house barking a greeting and promptly jumped up on the Chief.

"Coming!"

But he looked startled to see Digger on the front stoop. "Get down, Arthur! Shame! It's you."

"Expecting somebody?"

"Actually, I was. Am. Carla's on her way over. Come on in, I was just making coffee."

"You've heard about the second murder?"

"Second murder?"

"Felicity Shugrue. One of your brother's graduate assistants."

"Holy shit," Vance said. "Felicity Shugrue? Isn't she the little redhead, the one who was in Carla's weaving class?"

"Redhead, yes."

"Where? Not in the pit? When?"

"In that house she was renting out in the valley. When is still to be determined."

"How?"

"Messy. With a carving knife. I'm interviewing everybody who knows — knew — the deceased," Digger said formally, following Vance into the kitchen. "Both of them."

"Yes."

Carla arrived just then, bearing a loaf pan still warm from her oven and revitalizing the Dalmatian, who greeted her wildly. She fended him off with one hand while she set down the pan.

"Oh, good! You invited Digger."

"Not exactly. Tell her, Digger."

"The body of Felicity Shugrue was found on the floor of her kitchen early this morning. Run through with a carving knife."

"Dear God." Carla sat down at the kitchen table. "The little redhead? She came to my first class and then dropped out. Said she just had too much research work, she couldn't fit it in."

There was a long silence. Carla sat silently shaking her head. Digger drummed with his fingernails. Finally, Vance sniffed appreciatively. "God, that smells good!"

"Cranberry nut bread."

Vance poured three mugs, brought out the half-and-half and offered it to Digger, who hesitated.

"I'm on a diet."

"Skim?" said Vance.

"That would be great."

"I don't suppose you'll want a slice?" Carla said. "I'm afraid it's loaded with calories."

"You are breaking my heart," Digger told her. "Maybe half a slice."

"There you go," Vance said. "Do you think these two... murders are connected?"

Digger shook his head. "Too early to say." He took out his notebook. "Let's start with the message your brother got a couple of weeks ago. The one we found in his jacket pocket."

"You mean QUIT MONKS OR DIE?"

"Do you think that The Mercy Bandits...?"

Carla shook her head. "It's much too amateurish. The Mercy Bandits don't sit around cutting up magazines to make threats. They *strike*."

"Rachel made the note," Vance said. "She told me last

night, she cut out the letters from old magazines and put the thing in Hal's in-box in his office."

"Well, there goes that theory," Digger said. "You don't think The Mercy Bandits broke into the lab and stole the two missing monkeys?"

"If The Mercy Bandits had broken into Graysmith," Carla said drily, "there wouldn't be a monkey left in the place. There wouldn't be any records left."

"The monkeys are out at Joanna Hammerling's," Vance said.

Digger bit into his slice. "And who did that?"

"The twins. Apparently Rachel stole the keys from the custodian's keyring and she and Ben broke into the lab around midnight Sunday."

"Kids." Digger shook his head.

"And if The Mercy Bandits kidnapped the Director," Carla said, "they certainly wouldn't have left the body around to be discovered the next morning."

"The next morning? How do you know he was murdered the night before? The only two people who know the time of death are the Acting Medical Examiner and me."

Carla and Vance exchanged a long look.

"I know he was still alive Saturday night," Vance said.

"Yeah? How come?"

Without embellishment Vance described the kidnapping, the ladder, the sleeping bag and bread and water; the poncho and notebook and pen. And then his amazement when he went back to extricate his brother and found him gone.

"Vanished. Out of the pit," he finished.

"We'd talked about other ways to get him to give up these experiments," Carla said. "We wished we could exact a modern shaming, you know, like being put in stocks on the village green in front of all your neighbors?"

"But believe me, Hal could walk around in handcuffs in

front of the whole world and it wouldn't make a particle of difference to him. He was above behavior modification," Vance finished.

"Interesting that you should say handcuffs," Digger said. "That's what Fasher said about the body, that it looked as though it had been handcuffed."

"We had no intent to do bodily harm," Vance said. "We just thought we could get him to swear off, to give the monkeys up."

"And he did," Carla said. "Show Digger the note."

Vance fetched the handwritten disavowal, somewhat rain-spotted but legible.

It fit with what Fasher had said, that someone had been sequestered in the pit well before the body was discovered.

"You know this makes you liable for kidnapping, you could be charged under the law."

"We know."

"So who do you think got him out?"

Vance sighed. "I wish I knew."

"Carla?"

"I'm not sure. But I have a suspicion that it might have been a woman."

"Really? Why?"

"Well, for starters, I can't think of any man he knew who would go looking for him. Susie said he'd told her he was going into the canyon to their cabin."

"I've been up there already," Digger said.

"I wonder if he had some sort of…rendezvous planned for the weekend up there. The checkout woman at the Gourmet Superette — we were just making conversation last week while she added up my groceries — said Hal had been in there just the day before, buying some special items."

"Like what?"

"Oh, smoked oysters, I think she said. And caviar. Little

tins someone might put in a backpack."

"Any idea who he was planning to meet at the cabin?"

Carla shook her head.

"A student?"

"From what I've heard," Vance said, "it wouldn't be the first time."

"And who did you hear that from?"

"I'd rather not say."

"His wife?"

Vance nodded.

XXVIII

RICK ENSLIN SPENT most of Easter Sunday packing up his belongings. On one side of his narrow living room he made an orderly pile of papers, laptop powerbook, printer and the two cartons of textbooks in his field that he had amassed over the past few years. On the other he stacked his duffel and knapsack on top of the big leather suitcase now beginning to fray at the edges. It had been in the family as far back as he could remember, had accompanied him to college his freshman year and every year thereafter. He thought it would not withstand another trip.

In the late afternoon, having halfheartedly tidied the kitchen, he took a break and went outside to sit on a patch of grass in the spring sunshine. He pressed his big shoulders against the trunk of a liveoak and tried to fight down the hard cud of sorrow that sat in his throat. Ahead of him he saw an indeterminate sentence of once again working for his father. An indefinite period of mitred corners, of blueboard and lath. Miles of asphalt shingles overlapping just the right fraction of an inch. Calluses and bruised thumbs. Buckets of galvanized roofing nails. Bricks, mortar, cement blocks accompanied by a stream of oaths and imprecations until he could rearrange his life, re-enter a graduate program elsewhere.

Behind, this lotus-land of citrus trees and palms, the enormous desert yawning nearby. And Fifi.

Somehow he dozed off in the late slant of sun and came awake like a startled animal. Fifi. Before he packed the truck for the long trip back to Illinois he'd take a run out to her place to say goodbye, at least return the colander, the vegetable peeler and no-stick frying pan she'd loaned him from her wellstocked kitchen. If she hadn't gotten back from her weekend with friends, he could leave the utensils in the garage with a note.

In the haze of twilight Rick turned his Ford pickup down the gravel lane that led to Felicity's borrowed estate. An array of flowering bulbs rioted along the lane. Camellia bushes as tall as young trees were covered with deep burgundy blooms. To think he would leave this fecund irrigated place, to think he was going back to ice storms, late spring snows, another Midwestern mud season....

The little red Honda was parked out front. Good! Felicity was back. He pulled in behind her car, got out, and rang the doorbell. Nothing. He rang it again, this time laying his ear to the panel. Definitely on the fritz. He could hear the sound of running water, nothing else.

Shit. He'd said he would come over sometime and have a look. Why hadn't he? Probably a short circuit, a frayed wire. It was too cute anyhow, a doorbell that played Beethoven instead of a simple ding-dong. He tried the handle. Locked.

Around back, he saw the two fluffy Persians eyeing him through the kitchen window. The big gray one reached up a clawless paw and batted at a moth on the screen. Poor things, they didn't have much of a life in confinement. At least they had each other.

Wisteria climbed all over the back porch, hugging the supports as if to squeeze the life out of the already dead wood. He paused to take in the heavy perfume, rich and rank enough to make his eyes water. One more thing he was going to miss.

The back door was unlatched; he pushed it open and went in, then stood a long minute listening.

"Fifi?"

The bedroom door was open. In the light from the hallway Rick could see Hal face up and naked on the bed, his arms splayed, handcuffed to the fanciful wroughtiron tracery of the kingsize headboard. Fifi, wrapped in a bathtowel, bent over him, her mouth on his mouth. She lifted her head, pounded on his chest, crying, "Breathe, Hal! Please, please breathe!"

IXXX

Rick Enslin wasn't hard to find. In between Felicity's mother's frantic messages on the answering machine, Rick's voice addressed Fifi daily. He had apparently left at dawn on Monday, driven as far as Albuquerque and holed up in a Super 8 where he slept, he said, "on tissue paper sheets dreaming of you." Tuesday night he was on the outskirts of Oklahoma City; the weather was so warm that he pitched his pup tent in a KOA campground and slept under the stars. Wednesday took him through Kansas and into his home state, but it was too late at night to show up "on the doorstep," he told Felicity's machine, "so I just blew my stash on a half-decent motel where I can shower and shave before I play the part of the prodigal son." In this message he left Felicity his home phone number and begged her to call. Where the hell was she, anyway, three nights in a row?

Thursday night Digger dialed that number.

"This is Chief of Police Diego Martinez calling," he said. "From Montandino, California. I'm trying to reach a Mr. Rick Enslin."

"That's me."

"I'm afraid I have some bad news for you, Mr. Enslin. Very bad news. Do you know a Felicity Shugrue?"

"Fifi? Yes. Of course I know her, we're good friends. What's wrong?"

"I'm sorry to have to tell you this. She's dead."

"Dead? What do you mean, dead?"

"Murdered."

"She can't be! Who would murder her?"

"Her body was discovered very early this morning."

"My God! Where?"

"In the house," Digger said. "I'm sorry, I can't provide you with any more details. You'll have to come back."

"But I just got here."

"You are wanted for questioning."

"Questioning? You don't think... you can't possibly think I did it?"

"You are not being charged, Mr. Enslin. But you are possibly the last person who saw the deceased alive and you will have to provide us with a statement."

"But how do I get there? Who's going to pay my way?"

"You'll have to work that out on your own," Digger said. "At least for the time being. I assume you want to cooperate with the investigation? Otherwise, we'll have to issue a subpoena."

"A subpoena? What for? I didn't do anything!"

"That's why I need you here tomorrow, as early as you can make it. Depending on the evidence, you may have to be a grand jury witness."

It was only Digger's second homicide in thirty years. The first one had been a crime of passion when a cuckolded husband shot his wife. This time, with the Director and his graduate student, he was going to have to do some sleuthing.

❐

Rick flew in the following morning; his father, after bellowing and posturing like an enraged bull, had advanced him the air fare. Digger noted that Enslin was dressed in a black tee shirt and well-worn jeans. His sculpted body announced that he had been a college athlete, that he prided himself on staying fit. But the cant of his shoulders sent a different message.

"Take a seat," Digger said, keeping his tone neutral. "I think we're ready to begin." He fussed with the buttons on the machine. He hadn't used it much; he hadn't had frequent occasions to record interviews or confessions and the variety of things to push— record, rewind, fast forward, pause— made him nervous.

But before he could so much as turn on the tape recorder there was a knock on the door. He opened it, saw that his caller was Fasher, excused himself, stepped out into the hallway and closed the door behind him.

"What is it, Laurence?"

"Well, Dago, I'm on the way to the D.A.'s office with the path report and the autopsy results on Baranoff, and I thought I'd come by here first and share my conclusions with you in person."

"Which are?"

"Death due to autoerotic strangulation potentiated by intoxication and possibly triggered by heart attack."

Digger exhaled audibly. With those results no one could point a finger and say *murder*. "And the contusions and abrasions? The non-sexually inflicted ones?"

"These were sustained when the body was deposited in the pit."

"Good. Very good, Laurence. Thanks for ...sharing your conclusions." Digger allowed an edge of irony to creep into his voice. "And now, if you'll excuse me, I have work to do."

"Well, what are you going to do about it? If it wasn't a homicide, who abducted him? What about the suspicious circumstances?"

"Clearly I am going to do something. But since we're not looking at a homicide I'm going to think long and hard before I take action."

"But what about the evidence? The buttons done up

wrong, the blood alcohol content and so on? You're not going to suppress the evidence?"

"Of course not, Laurence. But let me tell you a little story."

"What kind of a story?"

"A true one. Once there was a very good governor of the state of New York."

"New York?"

"Before your time. Name of Nelson Rockefeller."

"So?"

"So he divorced his wife of twenty-five years and married his mistress and should have lived happily ever after."

"What happened?"

"He died in a strange hotel room in bed with a strange woman."

"Strangled?"

"Let's say he overexerted himself. Heart attack."

"I don't see what that has to do...."

"The particulars were not made public. The press was tuned down, muted. His wife's life was not shattered by scandal and he received a decent burial."

"So what you're saying is...."

"I'm not saying anything, that's the point. I'm not saying anything until all the facts are in, and I urge you not to say anything either. Goodbye, Laurence. Give my regards to the D.A."

❐

He and Rick sat across from each other in the Chief's cozy little office. It was a mild spring morning with a good breeze from the east. A mockingbird sang loudly and joyfully outside the window. Digger turned the tape recorder on, blew into it, said, "Testing, testing," hit the replay button, turned the volume down a little, and they began.

After Rick described finding Felicity Shugrue trying to resuscitate Dr. Baranoff, Digger asked, "Did you call 911?"

"No. Maybe I should've, but I tried to find a pulse and there wasn't any. He wasn't breathing, he was ...dead. I think he'd been dead for five minutes at least."

"What makes you think that?"

"Well, the doorbell wasn't working, so I went around back and fooled around for a while watching the cats, they were inside at the kitchen window batting at moths outside, then I kind of...lost myself in the wisteria, it's swallowing up the whole back porch, and then I found out that the kitchen door was unlatched. I let myself in and called Fifi but there wasn't any answer."

"And then?"

"I waited a while listening, and then I walked down the hall and looked into the bedroom and there she was."

"What did you think had happened?"

"I didn't have to think. I mean, I'd suspected from the beginning that they were having an affair, but she never came out and said so. She went crazy then, when she realized he was dead, all she could think about was getting rid of him, getting the body out of there so no one would know she'd been involved. She said a scandal involving her with Dr. B. would ruin her reputation, her entire career would go down the drain. It would ruin her reputation back in New Haven, too, and wreck her mother's life, she was an only child, her mother doted on her. All those things. She promised she'd be my...my girlfriend forever if I would help her now. She thought if we could just take him back to the pit where she'd found him, the monkey pit somebody had put him in, and let them think he'd... died down there, she thought we'd be... in the clear."

"Wait a minute. So she was the one who got him out of

the pit? When?"

"Oh, early that morning. She hiked back down from the canyon, that's where they were supposed to meet, to spend the weekend, and she went looking for him and eventually she located the pit of despair, she knew about it, a lot of us knew about it, but she didn't know exactly where it was, she just walked around out back and kept going and then she heard him calling and helped him get out and took him home to clean up, she said he was all muddy and furious, and then they drove back to her place, he was starving so she fixed him a big breakfast."

It all dovetailed with what Digger and Fasher had found in the Baranoff garage. "Did she happen to mention how she spent the rest of the day?"

"She said he was terribly... tired from the whole thing, she thought at the time that he didn't look well. He looked gray, almost. He wanted to take a nap."

"And what did she do then?"

"I guess she did a bunch of things, worked on an article she was revising for him. Then she messed around in the kitchen and read the Sunday papers."

"And then?"

"Well, around four o'clock she said he got up and she fixed a little platter of crackers and things and they sat in the living room and had some wine and cheese. He was very big on California wine, Fifi said he was a California wine chauvinist."

"And what do you think happened after the wine and ...crackers and things?"

"Well, I think they went to bed together."

"Did she ever talk to you about their...sex practices?"

"She never actually admitted they were having sex."

"Did you ever...have sex with her?"

Rick was silent.

"Yes?"

"We never had intercourse. She...helped me out occasionally."

"Are you a virgin?"

"Christ! No."

"Do you ever engage in S & M?"

"I was raised Lutheran," Rick said. "I'm not a prude but I don't need scarfs and handcuffs to get off."

"And Dr. B. did?"

"Apparently. And those capsules you crush and sniff at the last minute. Lots of stuff like that."

"Were you in love with Felicity Shugrue?"

"I would have been. If she'd given me any encouragement."

"Let's get back to the moment you discovered Felicity giving Dr. B. mouth-to-mouth resuscitation. Where had she been, do you think, while he was dying?"

"She said she left him the way she always left him, tied to the bed and pulling against the scarf as hard as he wanted to, she said that was the way he liked to ...come, make it last as long as he could. She got up the way she always did and went to take a shower."

"So she didn't tighten the scarf herself?"

"No. She said it was like play-acting, she acted one role and he acted another, there wasn't any harm in it."

"But as it turned out?"

"I can't believe any of this happened," Rick said. "I still feel like I'm walking through a dream somewhere. A nightmare."

"All right. Let's go through this one more time. Let's start over with what you saw, what you did."

"Well, I drove over to say goodbye to Fifi, I was... planning to leave the next day."

"To go where?"

"Drive back to Illinois."

"On holiday?"

Rick hesitated.

"We need the whole story."

"I was leaving for good. Dr. Baranoff had...dismissed me from the program two days before."

"Dismissed you?"

"Threw me out of the graduate program."

"On what grounds?"

"Trumped up. Said he had lost faith in my project, that there is no such thing as altruism in animals or in humans."

Digger looked bewildered. What the hell was altruism in humans? Something to do with welfare, he thought. Or something religious.

"That's what I'm writing my dissertation about, aspects of altruism in early childhood."

"So if he cashiered you from the program, that provides you with a motive."

"I know it looks that way. But I swear it doesn't. I didn't have anything to do with it. Him throwing me out of the program, it doesn't have anything to do with it. The reason he threw me out of the program was because Fifi and I were friends, he was afraid I was muscling in on him."

"But you weren't."

"I told you, she didn't give me the time of day."

"And after you were both sure Dr. B. was dead, how did you...transport him?"

"Fifi took the handcuffs off and we got him back into his clothes, which wasn't easy, let me tell you, and then we tried to figure out how to move him."

"How did you?"

"There's an old wheelbarrow in the tool shed, we put it in the bed of the pickup and then we put ...him in the back, too."

"Go on."

"Well, Fifi said wait, let's take a rake so we can rake over the tire tracks so we stopped and went back and she got this old bamboo rake with some teeth missing...."

"And you drove around the far side of Graysmith and wheeled the body in the wheelbarrow all the way to the pit. Damned near half a mile," Digger said. His tone conveyed admiration.

"Yes. It was terrible. We waited until it was pretty late, we were both in a panic that someone would see, somebody would call the police. Especially out there on the driveway when we were trying to lift the body out and get it into the wheelbarrow, you know, get it balanced so it wouldn't...keep tipping over. And the wheelbarrow was really hard to push, it just...bumped and jolted. I thought we'd never get there."

"And after?"

"Well, Fifi raked behind us all the way back out to my truck and we drove back here."

He didn't add: and for the first time she offered to let me make out with her. It was merely a payback. He didn't take her up on it.

"All right," Digger said. "And when you got back to Fifi's house, did you spend the night?"

"No. I left right after we got back, I just dropped her off and came back to my apartment, I still had to clean up some, sweep the place and so on. I wanted to get an early start. It's a long drive back, I was hoping to do it in two days and a little."

"What time would that have been?"

"I don't know exactly. It must have been close to midnight till we got...the body into the pit. So probably like one or two AM."

"Did you notice any other vehicles on the road, going

or coming?"

Rick hesitated. "Well, when I was driving out to Fifi's I remember seeing…at least I think it was him…Drew Deveraux's old pickup headed the other way. It looked like he was going out to the desert, maybe to Joanna Hammerling's."

"Did you acknowledge each other?"

"Yeah, well, he lifted a hand off the wheel and I did the same and then we passed by each other."

"How well do you know Deveraux?"

"About like everybody else in town, I guess. I knew him when I first came to Montandino, we had a beer together now and again. I didn't know anybody else in town and he acted like he didn't either. He was pretty good company once you got past all his… epithets."

"Epithets?"

"You know, calling everybody a whore or a white nigger or a stupid spic."

Digger stored the word for future use.

"Sometimes he came along when Fifi and I went to a movie. Once, he came with us to get a pizza."

"Is it possible he had a crush on Fifi?"

"I don't think Drew does girls," Rick said.

"So possibly you were the attraction?"

"He never made a pass at me. I mean, he never put his arm around me in the movies or anything. Look. The guy is lonely, he's probably dying of cancer, why shouldn't I buy him a beer and pizza?"

"Absolutely," Digger said. "Well, that's pretty complete, Mr. Enslin."

"Rick."

"Rick. I hope you're planning to stay around here a few days?"

"Yeah. Well, I was even thinking…since I wasn't ever

officially dropped from the program...maybe I'd stay a while and see if I could finish my dissertation."

"Good," Digger said. "Just leave me your local address and phone."

XXX

IT WAS HELL WASHING the blood off. He couldn't believe how much of it there was, how it spurted out and just kept coming and coming. He tried to get most of it off his hands and clothes while standing there, in her kitchen.

❐

But then he just went a little haywire, he had to get out of there and ran out to his truck, he'd left it down the road, parked on the other side, pulled in behind an old hay pavilion that was half falling down.

He drove back to Napara, reliving the whole nightmare: after he'd passed Rick going toward Fifi's house, he'd turned around and followed him. He'd crept around the outside the opposite way where he had a good view through the big windows, saw them struggle to get the Director's clothes back on him and the body out to the garage. Of course he knew where they were going, he'd known in the first place about the pit. He'd tailed Fifi down from the canyon at dawn that morning; it had been one of those sleepless nights and he hurt so much he was better off out cruising. He'd taken a run up to the canyon thinking to watch the sun rise, thinking he didn't know how many more of these he'd see, and sure enough, there was her little Honda and the Director's big fancy BMW, and then there she was, swinging along with her backpack as free and easy as an unbroke filly.

❐

She was filth. She deserved to die. Women like her always came to some bad end. At least Lottie only brought men home when she was drunk and sentimental, bawling, scared to be alone. This Fifi'd been fucking the Director, tying him down and riding him like a bucking bronc and she was about to fuck Rick who'd been his buddy, fuck him God knows how, God knows what sick things she'd teach him to do and God knows who else would come along to be fucked, only spics use knives, he did the right thing, it was the right thing, he did it for Lottie and for Rick.

XXXI

By the time Digger caught up with Drew Deveraux on Friday, he had been admitted to St. Vincent's. They'd already transfused him twice and were debating another pint.

"Bleeding internally," the resident told Digger. "Not a lot we can do for him at this point. Sure, you can go in."

He already had a visitor, a woman, who looked none too pleased to see him.

"Chief of Police Martinez," he said, offering his hand.

"Obviously," Joanna said. "In that uniform."

"You don't remember me, Mrs. Hammerling. But you had some runaway llamas a few years back. Got loose onto the highway?"

"Oh yes. And you went hightailing after them, flapping your cap at them like a drugstore cowboy, of course I remember."

"And Drew here, he was the hero, he got a rope around the one in the lead."

"He knew what he was doing," Joanna said drily. "You were a few pounds lighter back then."

"I was," Digger agreed. "I'm trying to lose weight but it seems like anything I eat, it goes right here." He patted his paunch.

"Well, now that we've got the civilities out of the way, what do you want? Why are you here?"

"I've come to question Drew about the murder. He needs to give me a statement, he's entitled to have a lawyer present."

"He doesn't have a lawyer. The way things are going, he doesn't need one."

"Well, I don't like to question him without counsel present...."

"You don't have any right to barge in here with questions. This is a very sick man, you can see for yourself. He's barely conscious."

"I can come back later," Digger offered. "But I need to interview him as soon as he's strong enough."

"You mean, once I leave, don't you? Well, you can hang around as long as you like, I'm not planning to leave."

Digger sighed. Joanna Hammerling was rightly famous not only for her reclusiveness but for her hard shell. He tried another tack.

"Has he said anything to you about the events... of the last few days?"

"He's been bleeding to death in his apartment for the last few days."

"Before that."

The body on the bed stirred. Drew opened his eyes. "Crank me up some, will you?" His voice was scratchy from disuse. "Some water?"

Joanna reached for the button and brought the head of the bed up a little. She held a straw to his lips.

"I did it," he said. "I had to do it, she was filth...."

"Wait, wait, I need to get this on tape," Digger hurried to start the recorder. He punched two buttons at once in his haste and then he had to rewind and start over. "Now can you just say that again?"

Drew murmured, "I did it."

"Get out," Joanna said.

"I'm getting, I'm getting. You're a witness to this confession. If a grand jury is convened, I may need you to give testimony."

"Get out, you nosy cop!"

Digger turned at the door. He saw that he had blundered

into a scene of excruciating intimacy and there was no dis-
creet way to extricate himself. Tears streamed down Joanna
Hammerling's face; her hands were two big fists in her lap.

"I'm very sorry," he said. "Goodbye." He closed the door
behind him as quietly as he could.

XXXII

No FUNERALS WERE HELD in Montandino. In the end, all three bodies were cremated. Felicity's ashes were shipped to her mother in New Haven. The poor woman was too distraught to fly to California to identify the body. Before it could be burned, Digger took Rick to the morgue to swear that the chalky white corpse under the sheet was indeed Felicity's.

There was a snappish moment with Fasher, who insisted that Rick should be charged for his part in failing to report a death and for transporting a body with intent to conceal it.

"Now, Laurence," Digger said, in the patient tone of voice he might use with a cluster of small children begging for candy, "suppose you tell me what the community will gain from my arresting this young man."

"But he committed a criminal act!"

"Remember what I told you a ways back about the governor of New York State? If I book this kid for any kind of criminal mischief, the whole story will have to be told. Then what you've got is a disgraced wife and a couple of kids who can't hold their heads up in public. To say nothing of what you do to the reputation of the Graysmith Lab, which employs half the people in this town."

"The law is the law," Fasher said.

"The law is designed to serve the whole body politic," Digger found himself saying, to his surprise. "I'm not about to see this town tied up in a nasty sex scandal just so your notion of justice is served. And let me point out that you're the Acting Medical Examiner. I take it you'd like to stay on as the actual Medical Examiner?"

Laurence grunted an affirmative.

"Well, I'm on good terms with the members of the commission that makes that decision. Excellent terms, you might say."

"I see your point," Fasher said.

"Shall we shake hands on it?"

◻

Before the end of the school year Vance moved in with Susie and the twins. They were discussing the possibility of moving back East. Vance had been offered a writer-in-residence position at a prestigious small college in Vermont. It came with a three-bedroom Victorian on Main Street. He was pretty sure it wouldn't be a replay of his year at Thoreau, but even if the students were all space cadets, at least the four of them would be together.

Susie, to her astonishment, had been tagged for an editorial job on *Food Thoughts*; she could drive down to Boston once a month or so for board meetings. Reuben was ready to start over. Marilyn could come to visit for Christmas, if they were still together. He was willing to sell his beloved VW and put the cash toward something suitable for driving the Vermont hills: a Saab, for instance.

It was hardest for Rachel. She and Amanda grieved endlessly about the separation. Worst of all, it meant leaving Magic behind. Susie pointed out that it didn't make sense to haul him three thousand miles to a new home in a strange cold climate. He'd already survived one trauma in his life; now he was happy and healthy, adjusted to his present environment. Rachel wept at the prospect. They would buy her a horse of her own in the north country, a Morgan, perhaps. Vermont was famous for its Morgan horses.

Each of them was silent, thinking about the late Harold Baranoff, husband, father, Director. Susie had saved his ashes. She thought she would like them to be interred on Long Island, in the family plot.

For now, they focussed on the trip east. Susie and Vance would sell their cars and buy a sports van with a popup camper to haul behind. The twins debated whether to choose the northern or the southern routes, ticking off the state parks they wanted to stay in en route.

❒

Early one morning in June before the day had heated up, Digger Martinez and Joanna Hammerling headed out of town on a bizarre errand. Digger was riding shotgun because what they were about to do was not only unusual but highly illegal. Joanna's tape deck played "O bury me not on the lone prairie..." as Drew had requested. Once they were on the interstate leading out to the desert, she rolled down her window and motioned for Digger to do the same. Then she handed him the cardboard box containing Drew's ashes. Gingerly he took a pinch of grit and bone and flung it behind him, out into the wind. She did the same. They took turns scattering the final remains of Drew Deveraux as they barreled into the sunrise.

KELLY WISE

ABOUT THE AUTHOR

Maxine Kumin is the author of twelve books of poetry, four novels, a book of short stories, three essay anthologies, and a number of children's books. She has received numerous awards including the Pulitzer Prize, the Poets' Prize, the Levinson Prize, and, most recently, the Ruth Lilly Poetry Prize. She lives and writes in New Hampshire.